ROLAND WINSALL
ASYLUM

For Marilyn, Ryan and Paige

Acknowledgements

I am so thankful to the following people who have supported me over this journey:

Robert Knox – an old friend, confidant and patient reader and reviewer of my many drafts, whose input and suggestions are always constructive and gratefully received.

My sisters, Sherry Hodson and Janine Sabec – two of my greatest supporters.

Friends and past work colleagues – Peter and Robyn Renner, Sue Munton, Ray and Jan Thomas, Carol Shaw and David Drill - much appreciated readers of my stories.

Special thanks to Jason Swiney and the team from Fontaine Publishing Group for their advice and expertise when getting this book to its final stage.

Prologue

Once the police investigation was over, and the media got bored reporting the murders, Nick visited the asylum where Dr Shelton had conducted his grisly experiment.

He spoke with Dr Paul Reading, Shelton's nemesis, who said he felt somewhat guilty – after all he was the one who had suggested the treatment in the first place. But Reading stressed that he'd told his audience of psychiatrists the treatment had not yet been approved by the medical board.

Nick asked him why Shelton had been so jealous of him, but Reading could throw no light on the matter. He just said he thought Shelton needed to be first and so he subjected that poor boy to the dreadful procedure without, it appeared, doing any research at all.

* * *

Aimtree House Private Hospital, or 'Aimtree Nut House', as the locals like to call it, stands majestically on a hill overlooking a winding green boulevard that snakes its way ever downwards to Melbourne's most famous waterway, the Yarra River. From the top of its bluestone buildings, it's possible to see the towers and skyscrapers that dominate Melbourne city, some five kilometres away.

Aimtree has been around for over a century. It was originally called 'Aimtree Asylum for the Insane' and then 'Aimtree Lunatic Asylum' but now, in a politically correct society, its name is more empathetic and makes it less obvious that, as a hospital, it cares for the mentally ill.

Numerous new wings have been added over the years, one for males and one for females, and other specialised units have also been built. But the main structure is still the original, sprawling three-storey edifice constructed in the Italianate architectural style popular back in the 1800s. The ground floor reception area has changed little over the past one hundred years. Dark timber columns and support beams surround the huge open space. The walls are painted a faded yellow and are dominated by large portraits of the Directors of Mental Health running back decades. It has always been a daunting place to enter and does little to put people at ease.

The second floor is an administration area for use by staff only. Patient records, held since Aimtree was first opened, are kept here, as well as a vast array of drugs and medicines all securely locked away. There is a small lunch area for the staff and a private room where the nurses can change from their street clothes into their uniforms.

The third floor has a chequered history. For years it was occupied by those poor souls who were completely insane and considered totally beyond help. After admission, they lived their whole lives in isolation on the third floor and only ever saw the outside world through the single window in their room. Rumours abounded in the local neighbourhood of the people that were held there. Stories were told of the worst patients being totally covered in hair, like a mixture of human and animal. They said they could hear them late at night screaming and howling at the moon.

These days the third floor has undergone significant renovations. The rooms have been upgraded and the ancient locks replaced with new stainless steel ones, but the doors are still very secure – locked from the outside. The third floor continues to hold those who are mentally ill, but now it's reserved for individuals convicted of violent crimes. It's especially designed for people who have been deemed by the courts to be criminally insane.

A high cyclone wire fence runs the full perimeter of the hospital. Most patients, except those who are too ill and those on the third floor, can move around and go outside. A select few are allowed to venture out past the fence. They are quiet souls and run no risk to society. They generally make their way down to the oval and sit there until it's time to return in the afternoon. On a few occasions a patient has disappeared for a day or two but they are easily tracked down. Some make it into the local shops where they are often found wandering aimlessly.

The grounds of Aimtree House are beautiful. There are extensive gardens and a full-time gardener. A large football oval is kept in perfect condition. The local school has permission to use it for interschool football matches, however the students are under strict instructions to never talk to the few patients who sometimes sit around the periphery.

A winding path runs from one side of the hospital grounds through the large car park and out onto the boulevard on the other side. It's possible for members of the public to use the path as a shortcut, but foot traffic is few and far between. Sometimes cyclists rush by, but they never stop.

Aimtree House is a quiet place, most of the time. The screams and yells that come from inside the buildings from those poor unfortunate individuals with their sick and tortured minds are generally well muffled by the hospital's thick stone walls.

Aimtree House might have changed its name to a hospital, but deep down everyone knows it is still a mental asylum.

Aimtree House is a place for the insane.

1

HEAT

For two weeks now the summer sun has baked the state of Victoria. The scorching temperatures have been relentless. North of the state is like a furnace that never shuts down; the ground is cracked and the crops are ruined. In Greater Melbourne it isn't much better. Apparently two weeks of 40-plus degree days is some sort of record, and the nights aren't that much cooler. No one can sleep. Everyone is hot, tired and restless.

The office blocks in the CBD are like giant ovens. Air conditioners run twenty four hours a day but only manage to lower the temperatures to a rank, clinging mugginess. In the open it feels as if the air itself is on fire. In some parts of Melbourne, the streets have started to melt – the bitumen reverting to a sticky black tar that threatens to hold fast anyone or anything that sets foot on it.

Trains arriving at Flinders Street Station have been reduced to walking pace as the tracks buckle and warp under them. Trams, packed with hot and sweaty passengers, threaten to rattle themselves apart as they groan along the roasting hot metal rails.

The weather bureau has been forecasting a break from the heat for days, but so far the hot northerlies have continued relentlessly. Everyone is waiting and praying for the cool change.

A long way to the west, in the Great Australian Bight, a giant low-pressure system is building. It's surrounded by several high-pressure systems – the perfect conditions for a storm.

Huge rain clouds are gathering and the giant system is growing ever bigger and slowly starting to spin. An enormous supercell is forming. The South Australian Weather Bureau has predicted that the system will head east and is likely to sweep across the whole state of Victoria. The devastation could be massive.

There is a storm on the way – a giant storm – and nothing can stop it.

2

MURDER IN SOUTH MELBOURNE

10:00pm and she was finally home; it had been another long day at work – too long. At least the twenty-minute drive from her nursing job at the hospital to her house in South Melbourne was easy. The traffic this time of night was always light.

She parked her car in the driveway, got out, unlocked the ancient garage door and struggled to lift it. Inside the car it had been cool with the air conditioner running flat out, but now she was outside, the air was super-heated even this late at night, and felt as if it would burn her if she stayed out too long.

Overhead the dark night sky was lit with a million stars. A gusting northerly picked up again and tossed the shadowy bushes lining the driveway back and forth. It lifted her hair and whipped it across her face. She tucked it behind her ears with sweaty hands.

She drove the car in, got out, locked it and went back outside, then stretched up and grabbed the garage door. With an effort, she pulled it down and twisted the key in the lock. She entered her small two-bedroom weatherboard house through the front door, not noticing the broken window in the bedroom facing the street. The curtain had snagged on a jagged shard and was flapping out into the night as though trying to get her attention – to warn her!

Inside, she turned on the lights, switched on the evaporative cooler and opened the fridge. She brought out a bottle of sav blanc, now half empty after the glass or two she'd had the night before. She got a wine glass from the kitchen counter and poured herself a good measure. She took a sip of the chilled sour alcohol then walked over to the couch in the lounge room, flopped down and grabbed the TV remote control. The television sprang into life as she nestled into the cushions.

The volume from the television covered any noise made by the dark shadow that emerged from the hallway and stood behind her – a hammer swinging back and forth easily in one hand.

'How was your day?' came a whisper from behind.

She sat up with a jolt half looking at the TV before she craned her neck around.

'Oh my God!' she said as she sucked in air.

The tall figure towered over her. She spilt the glass of wine as she stood up.

'Who are you?' she said. 'What … What do you want?' Her hands shook and her heart started beating at a million miles an hour.

'Tonight you're going to get it, bitch!'

'W-w-what?' she stammered and started to walk backwards.

The tall figure shouted, 'There's no sense running! It's way too late for running!' and climbed over the couch towards her.

The hammer swung in a deadly arc and came down on her skull, splitting it from her crown to the bridge of her nose. The force of the blow knocked her backwards and she staggered and tripped over the glass coffee table, shattering it into a thousand pieces as she crashed to the lounge room floor.

The ominous form stood over her, waiting to see if she would move. She didn't.

The next five blows of the hammer were brutal, turning her head to mush. Thick red spatters covered the opposite wall and blood began pooling under her body and soaking into the beige-coloured carpet, turning it a deep, deep red.

The hammer was cleaned on the nurse's blouse. She was rolled onto her back and undressed from her waist up. She lay there, semi-naked, dead eyes staring towards the ceiling. The flash from the mobile phone camera lit up the room as three photos were taken from different angles, showing her shattered face and small bare breasts.

The figure rummaged through her handbag, found a bright red lipstick and scrawled, *Way too late for running!* across the full length of the flickering television screen.

3

NICK JARRATT

On the sixth floor of the old Nicholas Building on Swanston Street in the centre of Melbourne, Nick Jarratt leant back in his chair and stared out at St Paul's Cathedral across the road. The church spires glinted in the blazing afternoon sun as they reached upwards towards a heaven that many hoped existed, but, given dwindling church attendance, fewer and fewer believed in. Down below a tram rattled past as it made its way across the intersection of St Kilda Road and Swanston Street – the busiest tram route in the world. He slowly swung his chair around behind his desk and peered through the glass panel of his office door into the small reception area. The sign on the outside read:

NICK JARRATT
PRIVATE INVESTIGATOR

Nick had taken a lease that included two adjoining offices. He occupied the one closest to the street, while

Rosalie, his receptionist, sat closest to the lift. It was hot on the sixth floor. The old air conditioner that Nick would swear on a stack of bibles was built in the 1960s blew a faint breeze into the offices, but by the time it reached their occupants the air was warm and stale.

Nick always had high hopes for the job. He thought it would present plenty of intrigue and challenges. But to date the only work he'd had was looking into insurance fraud or petty embezzlement in large companies. He hadn't even been hired by an older woman trying to catch her husband having it off with some young floozy. To date, his clients were mainly bald-headed accountant types, or stiff suits from audit departments trying to chase down a few missing thousands. The best he could hope for was that one of them had some idea who was committing the fraud so he could run surveillance on some poor unsuspecting white-collar criminal.

He could see Rosalie as she busied herself on her mobile phone, no doubt doing more online shopping. Work was slow, and if this downturn in the market continued Nick didn't know how much longer he could keep her on. He'd hired her as a favour for his best mate, Detective Pete Drury, who'd told him that Rosalie was the wife of one of his friends. She'd lost her job as a secretary for a law firm about the same time as she was splitting up with her husband. While the husband and Rosalie didn't get on anymore, Drury said he wanted to make sure that Rosalie was okay. Nick thought it sounded a bit odd but told Drury he'd put her on – as a favour to him.

Nick owed him one, actually he owed him much more than one. He first met Drury when they were in the police force together. They both made detective at the same time and things were looking good, that is until Nick completely stuffed it up. But Drury didn't desert him, in fact he helped Nick get his Private Investigator's licence when he was in his darkest hour.

Nick hit the intercom button.

'Hey Rosalie, we got anything on today?'

'Nothing yet Nick. I'll let you know if something turns up,' she said and went back to her phone.

'Okay, thanks Rosalie.' He took his finger off the button.

He leant back in the chair, put his hands behind his head and his feet up on the desk. He remembered his first meeting with her.

'Hi Rosalie, welcome to the *ranch*, I hope you like it here!'

'Thanks Nick, I really appreciate you putting me on.'

Rosalie was in her early forties and dressed in smart business clothes. She wore minimal makeup and a light-weight necklace. Nick noticed she wasn't wearing a wedding ring, but it was clear from the pale skin on her ring finger that she had for a very long time.

'Pleasure Rosalie,' he said. 'Look I've only just started the business recently, so there's not that many clients, and things can be a little slow at times.'

She nodded her head.

'I'm sorry, but there's no minimum wage, and some weeks things might be a little tough!'

Rosalie smiled at Nick with big, brown, sorrowful eyes. 'That's okay Nick, I'll manage. Thank you so much for giving me a chance.'

'Not a problem Rosalie,' Nick said and showed her to her desk at reception.

As it turned out it was one of the best things Nick could have done. Rosalie was fantastic. She had the office in shape in no time. Her filing system was great. She got in maintenance men to look at the CCTV, which hadn't worked since Nick had set the place up. She also organised for the backup battery for the alarm system to be replaced. She took over Nick's computer system and put together a spreadsheet that included all his clients, the reasons they had engaged Nick, payments made and any outstandings. She was incredible!

If anything, after twelve months or so, she was probably too good. While they got on well, Rosalie got to know most of Nick's vulnerabilities, and often, just for a bit of fun, she would exploit them.

4

TWO WOMEN CAN ONLY MEAN TROUBLE

Nick snatched a sheet of paper off his desk, screwed it up into a ball and threw it at the miniature basketball ring hanging on the opposite wall. He kept it there for when his son Liam visited, which wasn't all that often.

Liam only turned up when Nick's ex-wife, Angie, dropped him off and went shopping in the city. But at least he got to see the boy for a short while, and now that he was eight years old he could have some sort of sensible conversation. The dialogue with his wife, however, was a lot less friendly. It was always the same: tense, terse and hostile.

Nick and Angie had been boyfriend and girlfriend since high school, and in those early days everyone thought they'd be together forever. Things seemed to be following their natural path when they got married in their late twenties. They bought a house in an inner suburb of Melbourne and started putting down roots. After a couple of years Angie fell pregnant with Liam and Nick could see his life stretching out in front of him. He'd already done five years in the force and been promoted to detective. His prospects were bright. But then everything changed.

After the birth of Liam, Angie had trouble coping with the newborn. Nick could see things were getting worse and so he took paternity leave to help out. But as time wore on she became more distant. Nothing he did seemed to be right. They started to argue and Nick could see it was upsetting their young son. They began eating meals separately and eventually he took to sleeping in the spare bedroom. To avoid the constant fights he often worked long hours at the station and told Angie not to bother cooking for him anymore; he'd get his own. Actually, this wasn't a hard choice for Nick, as his favourite haunt was Young & Jackson on the corner of Flinders and Swanston streets. It did great food upstairs in the brasserie and there was also the full-length painting of Chloe, the innocent and naked pre-World War One beauty whose famous body had graced the hotel since 1909. Disastrous as his time with Angie had been, the painting always reminded him of her.

But it all changed for Nick. As things got worse on the home front, and he started to spend more and more time at the cop shop, his life took a turn for the better. It happened when a new intake of probationary constables started and one of the newbies, Claudette Morgan, caught his eye. She was petite, blonde, pretty and just a little naive.

* * *

Inside the cop shop Pete Drury nudged Nick, who looked up at him from checking posts on his mobile phone.

'Here come the Greenhorns!' he said as a group of newly graduated police officers walked in.

Nick glanced up but then went back to his phone.

'Looks like the quota system is workin',' Drury added. 'Half blokes and half young chicks!'

Drury's comment got Nick's attention. He looked up and saw Claudette. She noticed him looking at her and there was an instant connection.

'We'll probably each have to take one under our wing and show them the ropes. You know, wet nurse them and …'

Nick didn't wait to hear the rest of what Drury had to say. Instead he got up, walked over and introduced himself to the pretty blonde.

'Hi,' he said and held out his hand. 'I'm Nick.'

'Oh hi,' she said and took his hand. 'Claudette.'

'First day, hey?'

'Yes!'

She looked around the inside of the station and bit her bottom lip.

'Bit daunting! But don't worry I'll show you around.'

'Oh! thank you,' she said and smiled at him.

Nick made sure it was him that helped Claudette get acquainted with how things ran in the cop shop. They worked together from day one, and it was obvious to the others at the police station that they were *friendly*. It was only a couple of months later that Nick asked her out for a drink after work. She accepted and he took her to Young & Jackson.

* * *

Nick bought the drinks and they sat together on high stools at a raised table in the main bar. It was busy, but not too noisy.

'I just realised I never got to ask you where you live,' Nick said and smiled. He took a sip of beer.

He hoped he wasn't being too pushy but he had to know if she was attached.

'In an apartment in Carlton. I live there by myself.' She smiled at Nick, turned her head slightly, then took the slightest sip of her vodka and lemonade.

Nick's heart jumped. He was still married. He knew he shouldn't stray, but things had changed so much at home and he couldn't help but be infatuated by this beautiful young woman.

'Oh,' he said, trying not to seem too pleased with her response.

'What about yourself?' she asked.

He hesitated. This could make or break a promising re-lationship.

'At home … But things are not going well.'

Nick told her about the situation with Angie and the

trouble he was having. It all just tumbled out of his mouth. Claudette sat there and listened while Nick told her everything.

She waited for him to finish, then looked directly into his eyes and asked, 'Do you still love her?'

Her eyes never left Nick's as she waited for him to answer.

He hesitated. 'No,' he heard himself say.

His response hit him hard. He hadn't confronted this question before. Until now he had continually pushed it into the background. He always thought that he loved Angie, and would do so forever, but now that it was out in the open, and he'd actually spoken the word, he finally knew he no longer had feelings for her. It was a shocking truth for Nick, but it was as though a massive weight had been lifted off his shoulders. Having said it out loud made it final. He was surprised by his own reaction, but deep down he was pleased to have finally admitted it.

Claudette took another sip of her drink and didn't speak. Nick reached over and touched her hand. He wondered how she would react. It was the first time, apart from a cursory handshake, that they had touched each other. Claudette smiled at him, lifted one finger and placed it over his.

The after-work drinks continued for the next few months and soon rumours of their relationship started to do the rounds at the station. Dinners at Young & Jackson in Chloe's Brasserie led to movies afterwards. Ultimately Claudette took him back to her place and it wasn't long before Nick began staying the night, and the sex became as regular as clockwork.

Soon, however, things would come to a grinding halt.

5

GOOD TIMES, BAD TIMES

Coventry Street, South Melbourne, was the scene of a murder late at night. They found the victim, a woman in her thirties, in the lounge room of her modest two-bedroom home. She'd been bludgeoned to death with a blunt instrument, but by the time the cops got there the murderer was long gone.

She was naked from the waist up, however there were no obvious signs of sexual assault. Word came down the line that forensics wouldn't be there until the morning so the crime scene had to be preserved. Nick and two other detectives were rostered on as one team, while a second uniformed team in a divvy van was also sent, just in case there was an arrest and they needed somewhere to lock the suspect up. Sergeant Chris Tainsby drove the divvy van while Probationary Constable Claudette Morgan rode with him in the passenger's seat.

It looked like being a long, hot night. An hour into the wait, Tainsby got a call that his wife was sick and he had to get home to look after her. He gave Claudette the keys and said he'd be back in the morning.

The three detectives, Nick, Pete Drury and Grant Davidson, were seated in an unmarked police car outside the murder house half a block up from the divvy van. Nick sat in the back seat, Drury and Davidson in the front.

Drury finished his cigarette and flicked the butt out the open window.

'You have anything special on tonight Nick?' he asked as he stared out at the dark road ahead.

'No, nothin', what about you?'

'Bullshit!' Davidson spat out. 'You've always got somethin' special on, haven't ya Jarratt!'

His harsh comment and innuendo weren't lost on Nick, who didn't answer.

'You got that little piece of fluff, Claudette, haven't ya!' Davidson chuckled. 'Needs dustin' all the time, hey Jarratt!'

Davidson let out a sharp laugh.

Nick wasn't going to bite but could feel himself getting angry. He and Davidson had never got on. All three of them had started in the force at the same time, but Nick and Drury had been promoted before Davidson and he'd never gotten over it.

Nick opened the door.

'I'm goin' out to stretch my legs and have a look around.'

He didn't wait for the other two to comment. He couldn't get out of there quick enough.

Davidson smiled, pleased with himself. He bummed a cigarette from Drury, lit up and went back to staring out at the empty road.

Nick walked over to the house where the murder had taken place. He opened the gate and looked in the front yard. There was not much chance of finding anything worthwhile in the gloom, but he just wanted to get away from Davidson and his smart-arsed comments. He didn't want to risk disturbing anything so he stepped back onto the pavement and closed the gate again. He looked down the road and saw the divvy van and decided to walk towards it. As he got closer, he could see Claudette and noticed she was alone. His heart started racing as he walked over and knocked on the window.

'Hey, fancy seein' you here,' he said and leant on the side of the van.

Claudette had moved into the driver's seat and rolled down the window.

'Didn't know you were gonna be here,' she replied and smiled up at him.

'Where's your partner?'

'Had to go. Sick wife.'

'Oh, so it's just you, all by yourself?'

'Uh huh. You wanna keep me company?' she said and motioned with her eyes towards the passenger side.

Nick looked up the road at the unmarked police car.

'Sure. You know, all I've got to do is look at an empty house for the next ten hours!'

'Oh, don't you complain, I have to be here too!' she said and her smile got wider.

Nick walked around to the passenger side of the van and got in. He put his hand out and held hers.

'Did they see you walk down here?' she asked and looked out through the windscreen at the car up ahead.

'Not sure. I don't think so. They're too busy just lookin' at the road. Nothing will get past those two!' Nick said and laughed.

She looked out at the night then leant across in the seat and kissed him on the cheek.

'You wanna be naughty?' she said and looked up at Nick and bit her bottom lip. 'I've got the key to the back.'

Claudette dangled the divvy van keys in front of Nick. The adrenaline hit his stomach like a sledgehammer. He knew he shouldn't, but when he looked at her his self-control melted away like ice cream in the hot sun. He checked up the road one more time to make sure the other detectives weren't looking. Then he gently pulled her close and kissed her full on the mouth.

'Sure Claud!' he said as he drew away.

She rolled her eyes and smiled at him. Nick watched as she got out and walked to the back of the van, unlocked the door and swung it open. He waited a moment then followed her. As he pulled the door closed behind him he could see it was going to be a tight fit, but he figured they wouldn't be in there for that long.

'We'd better be quick!' he said as he undid his trousers.

She was soon naked and the smell of her perfume overwhelmed him. He was ready in a moment.

'I'm only as quick as you ever let me be!' she whispered and spread herself underneath him.

He kissed her bare breasts and within moments found his way inside her. His thrusting at first was slow and rhythmic, but he couldn't keep it in check and soon it became uncontrollable. The van started rocking and when she reached orgasm she let out a shriek, which was just a little too loud.

Pete Drury heard the noise and looked back down the road at the divvy van and saw it moving. Davidson looked across at Drury with a worried expression and then at the empty back seat.

'Jarratt's not back! Where is he?'

'Dunno!' Drury replied and flung open the passenger side door. 'Come on we'd better check this out!'

Davidson was slow and grunted as he edged his way out the driver's side.

'Shit, maybe they've arrested someone!' he said.

But Drury didn't hear him, he was already on his way.

Both detectives drew their handguns and ran down the road to the back of the divvy van. Drury was there first and swung the door open. Nick and Claudette were still entwined in their lover's embrace.

'Are you guys okay ...?' Drury just stood there, open

mouthed. He couldn't believe his eyes.

Davidson arrived a few seconds later. A leering half-smile spread on his face as he checked out the naked Claudette.

'Close the bloody door!' Nick yelled.

* * *

Back at the cop shop it was the hottest topic of conversation. There was a lot of smirking and talking behind hands. Nick had to face the station Commander. Things didn't go well. Drury tried to put in a good word for him but it fell on deaf ears. Davidson was pleased to watch proceedings from the sidelines. He couldn't have been happier as he watched Nick's downfall.

Within twenty-four hours Claudette was sacked, but fortunately for Nick, he was allowed to resign without a blemish on his record. Apparently the 'boys club' that had thrived for decades in the police force was still alive and well.

When Angie learnt of the affair she immediately filed for divorce. Her lawyer was slick. He knew that when he told the court it was Nick who had strayed, the cards would fall in his client's favour. He was right of course, and the settlement didn't go well for Nick. He lost more than half of the joint assets. Angie got the house and half of his superannuation and full custody of Liam. Nick was left with not much more than his wardrobe of clothes, which included a couple of suits and some jeans and tee shirts. There was just enough cash left over for him to rent a one-bedroom apartment in Flinders Street.

But at least the apartment was roomy and on the first floor, away from the direct rumble and clatter of the trams and other road noise. It resembled a barn more than an apartment. The only separate rooms were the bedroom and the bathroom, which backed onto a rickety fire escape. But it did boast its own private lift, which, noisy as it was, ran from the ground floor and opened directly into the apartment itself.

Finances soon became top of mind and Nick badly needed to find a job. It was during a late-night drinking session with Drury that a few different ideas were floated.

When the small talk was over Drury asked, 'So, how's it goin' Nick? What have you been doin'?'

Drury drained his stubby, walked over to the fridge, grabbed two more and handed one to Nick.

'Finances are running low, Pete,' Nick said. 'Gotta find somethin' to do.' He took a mouthful of the icy cold beer then said, 'Police work's the only thing I've ever done.'

Drury nodded, thinking. 'You can't sing or dance, can ya?' he asked and lifted his eyebrows.

Nick eye-fucked him.

'Word is, they're paying big bucks for male strippers down St Kilda way!'

Nick double eye-fucked him.

Drury smiled then took a long draw from the stubby.

'You know what, Nick. I just had a thought.'

'What?' Nick said, waiting for Drury's next crap joke.

'You remember Patterson, the old sergeant from the cop shop?'

'Yeah, he retired didn't he?'

'Yeah,' said Drury. 'Retired from the force, but set himself up as a Private D. The boys are saying he's doin' really well for himself.'

Nick stared at Drury. 'Really? What's involved in doin' that?'

'Well, I know you've gotta get a Private Investigator's licence, and there's some other crap as well that you need to get.'

Nick nodded, considering what Drury had suggested.

The drinking session went on for another couple of hours. When Nick woke up the next morning his mouth felt like it had been rubbed inside with a very dirty bar towel. He looked around, but Drury was long gone.

He grabbed a can of Coke out of the fridge, snapped the top, took a sip and screwed up his eyes as the fizz took over. Then he found his laptop, sat down at the kitchen table and looked up 'How to obtain a private investigator's licence'. He spent the next hour working his way through the search results and made some rudimentary notes.

Nick knuckled down when it came time to study and in a little over six months got the Certificate in Investigative Services from the local TAFE. Then he also applied for, and received, a Private Investigator's licence.

During this time, he also contacted the police super-annuation board and, on hardship grounds, requested a lump sum from his meagre superannuation balance. It was just enough for him to take out the lease on a rundown two-room office on the sixth floor of the Nicholas Building.

Finally, almost twelve months to the day that he'd been kicked out of the police force, he set up his Private Investigator business.

And it was only two days after that when he received the first child maintenance invoice from his ex-wife's solicitor!

6

BAD DREAMS

Nights were tough for Nick after being drummed out of the police force and the subsequent divorce. Sleeping alone was bad enough, but now he was starting to have regular bad dreams. The first ones seemed to replay the terrible arguments he'd had with Angie and the yelling and shouting. Others were more related to the police force and Davidson's leering face, plus the humiliation of being made to leave. Now, however, in the sweltering heat that hung over the dark city, a new dream kept coming to him, and this one was terrifying.

It's as though Nick is watching a movie of himself walking down a deserted city street. Maybe it's Swanston Street, but he can't be sure. It's late and one or two streetlamps throw a dim, gloomy light on the surroundings. He's lost. He keeps walking, though. He knows there's a place he has to be. He thinks it's somewhere down a lane, or maybe in a basement. He keeps hearing footsteps behind him, but each time he looks around there's no one there. He's being followed, he's sure of it. He walks faster and can now hear the footsteps keeping pace with him. He looks around again but can't tell if there's a dark figure hiding in the shadows. He gets to the corner of what looks like Swanston and Flinders streets. He stands out the front of St Paul's Cathedral and looks up across the road to his office. He can see Rosalie standing in the window staring down at him, yelling noiselessly and gesturing wildly. She's pointing behind him but Nick can't make out what she's saying. He looks around, and in the gloom, someone ducks out of sight.

He runs into the cathedral and hides behind one of the giant pillars. He looks up at the massive ceiling. Gargoyles with their ugly leering faces peer down at him. He's there by himself. He runs to a pew and hides. He stays perfectly still as he hears footsteps slowly enter the cathedral. Each solitary step echoes loudly on the cold flagstones. His heart is pounding.

Now he's outside again and running across the road and onto Flinders Street. The footsteps behind him are heavy. They're close! He runs past Young & Jackson and sees that the doors are locked. A picture of the naked Chloe flashes by.

A voice starts to talk to him, softly at first –

No sense running!

It gets louder –

It's too late for running!

Then it screams –

WAY, WAY TOO LATE FOR RUNNING!

Nick bolts down a darkened stairway taking the steps two at a time. It might be the tunnel that runs under Flinders Street and out to the railway station on the other side of the road. The further down he goes, the darker it gets. He's terrified of tripping in the darkness and has to slow down to try and see the stairs.

Now the footsteps are directly behind him. He jumps as a heavy hand grabs his shoulder and spins him around. He looks directly into the face of …

'Nooooo!' Nick yelled as he woke and sat bolt upright in bed.

He was covered in a heavy sweat and gulped down great lungfuls of the thick night air.

The illuminated glow of the bedside clock radio showed 2:38am.

Outside, a great northerly gust rattled the apartment windows, almost as though the tail end of the dream itself had finished with him and the night was passing on.

7

MISSING STEPBROTHER

The paper ball hit the backboard, ran around the rim and fell off to the side where it landed on the floor and nestled amongst a dozen or so others. Nick was about to check his phone when he noticed someone talking to Rosalie. He tapped a button on his laptop and the CCTV image in the reception area was immediately replicated on his computer screen. It was a tall woman. Within a minute Rosalie buzzed the intercom.

'Nick, someone here to see you.'

'Thanks Rosalie, send them through please.'

He took his feet off the desk and moved a bunch of papers around trying to give the impression of some semblance of order. The tall, well-dressed woman walked through the door. She had long auburn hair partially covered by a flimsy white headscarf. Draped over one arm was a dark green overcoat.

Why would she need an overcoat in this sort of weather? he wondered.

Her ruby red lipstick shone out vividly against her pale white skin. Her eye shadow was elegant, and made her emerald green eyes shine. She was a stunner. Nick could hardly believe his eyes.

'Mr Jarratt?' she said.

'Ah … yes! Please. Take a seat.'

She hung the coat over the back of the visitor's chair. Nick noticed she held a Louis Vuitton handbag with a beautiful pair of thin white gloves draped over the latch. He did his best not to stare at her ample cleavage as she sat down.

'How can I help you, Miss …?'

'Downton, Jessica Downton.'

He noticed that she started to wring her hands, as though giving her name was a major concession. She opened her handbag, took out a small handkerchief and dabbed at her eyes.

'Are you okay?' Nick asked, concerned.

'Yes, thank you,' she answered, then folded up the handkerchief and clutched it tightly. 'Mr Jarratt,' she paused and stared briefly out the window. 'I've come about my brother – my stepbrother actually. He's missing. I have no idea where he is. I need someone to find him.'

A tram rattled past and shook the window facing the street. Nick looked at her. There was a desperate note in her voice. She looked very anxious, but he guessed this was normal for someone who had a missing relative. Yet there was something else, something he couldn't quite put his finger on.

'Okay. So, your stepbrother, what's his name?'

'Alex … Alex Downton.'

Nick grabbed a fresh work contract and began to jot down some details.

'Downton, you said?'

He spelt out the surname and looked up at her for confirmation.

'Yes, that's right,' she said.

'Have you notified the police?'

She looked at him with a worried expression on her face.

'No,' she said softly.

'Oh. Why not?' Nick asked, surprised.

'They, ah … they … I don't trust them. I don't want them involved!' She spat the last comment out and her eyes flashed.

Nick leant back in his chair startled by her sudden outburst.

'Has he committed a crime?' he said, hoping not to antagonise her.

'No,' she replied as her tears started again.

'Is he likely to?'

She dabbed at her eyes.

'I don't know!' she said. 'I hope not! I don't think he will.'

A prickle of caution ran through Nick's brain as he paused for a moment to give her time to compose herself.

'How old is your stepbrother, Miss Downton?'

'He's eighteen.'

Nick made some notes.

'And where does he live? Have you checked there?'

It was a stupid question, he thought, but one worth asking.

She sat bolt upright. 'Yes of course I have! Do you think I'm an idiot?'

'No, no. Sorry. I know it's a dumb question.'

'He lives with me!' she replied and stared at Nick. Her beautiful eyes were glistening.

'So when did you last see him?'

'A week ago.'

As she said this she averted her eyes and Nick thought she might be lying but jotted the information down.

'A week ago?' Nick repeated, testing her.

'Uh huh,' she said and nodded, but didn't meet Nick's gaze.

'And was he with you up until then?'

She slumped back into the chair and shook her head.

'No … not really, I only spoke to him on the phone.'

'Oh okay,' Nick said, then added, 'did he give you any idea where he might be?'

'Not exactly, but I think he was in Melbourne some-where. I'm sorry. I haven't got any more than that.'

An uneasy feeling came over Nick as he looked at her.

'Is it usual for him to go away for that length of time?'

She hesitated, then looked up at Nick with pleading eyes.

'No. He isn't supposed to go away at all … he's supposed to … to stay with me.'

Nick gave her another moment before he went on.

'Is he likely to go interstate?' He probed a bit further.

She shrugged her shoulders.

'I doubt it, he doesn't know anyone interstate. He's …' she didn't finish the sentence.

Nick made more notes.

'Does he have a friend, or friends where he might go?'

She hesitated again.

'He doesn't have any friends. He only has me!'

Nick stared at her. This was getting stranger by the minute.

'Does he have any favourite places where he likes to hang out?'

She shook her head.

'Is he on any medication?'

'No,' she said and turned her head away.

Nick had the feeling she was lying again.

'Does he take drugs?'

'What?' She became defensive. 'He's never taken drugs in his life!'

'Okay, okay,' Nick said. 'I'm sorry, but I have to ask these questions, they might help.'

He tried another tack.

'Do you have a photograph of him?'

She dug around in her handbag and brought out a small photo of a young man and handed it over. He wasn't smiling. In the background Nick could see a huge three-storey building that ran from one side of the photo to the other. He thought he'd seen it before but couldn't be sure.

'How long ago was this taken?' he asked.

'About a year or so ago,' she replied.

'Can I keep it?'

'Yes,' she said and stood up. 'So, do you think you can help?'

'Yes, yes, I think so. This is right in my line of work, but I'd like to ask you a few more questions.'

'Good … But I'm sorry, I can't stay any longer. I have to go.'

She put on the pair of thin white gloves, picked up her handbag and took her coat off the back of the chair.

'Do you have a number where I can contact you?' he asked.

'Yes, but I always check the caller ID first. I don't like to answer it. Not often, anyway. If I don't like the person calling, I don't answer at all!'

She looked at Nick suspiciously. He felt a little uneasy under her gaze as she took a pen off his desk and jotted down her number on a yellow sticky note.

'Why don't you like to answer it?' Nick asked, curious.

'I only ever get bad news. I hate it!' she snapped, glaring at Nick.

A look of concern crossed Nick's face.

'Look before you leave, I need you to sign this. It's a work contract. My rates are seventy-five bucks an hour, all billable. More if it's after hours and double time on the weekends. The paperwork is fully detailed. I'll record exactly what I've done every month – if the investigation goes that long.'

She took the work contract and scribbled her signature on the bottom of the document.

'Do you need a payment now?'

'No. The first visit is free,' Nick responded, smiling.

He handed her his card. 'You can call me any time during office hours for an update.'

'I'd prefer to come here in person once a week if that's okay?'

'Sure, not a problem.'

'I can pay you then.'

'Okay,' Nick said, 'that'll be fine, I'll show you out.'

'No need,' she said.

With that she turned, opened the door and walked through the reception area and over to the lift. Nick watched as the doors closed behind her, then sat down and began reading the brief notes he'd made. He was halfway through when the intercom buzzed.

'Hey Nick, who was that?' Rosalie asked.

'It was a Miss Downton, Rosalie. Jessica Downton.'

'What did she want?'

'Her stepbrother's missing.'

'How'd you know she was a Miss?'

'No ring on her wedding finger,' he said, a bit exasperated. 'Look, Rosalie, can you just come in here and load this new work contract into the system please!'

'Okay Nick. Do you like her?'

'What!'

'Come on, Nick, I saw the way you looked at her, she's very pretty. What will Claudette think if she finds out?'

'There's nothing *to* find out Rosalie! Jessica Downton is a client, and that's that!'

Nick was getting angry. Rosalie was pushing his buttons again and having a bit of fun with him. He heard her snigger as she clicked off the intercom.

Nick had stayed in touch with Claudette ever since the divvy van incident. He really liked her, but wanted to make sure the relationship was just casual. He didn't want to get tied down again like he had with Angie. He told himself it was still okay to look around, and he did have to agree with Rosalie that Jessica Downton was a very attractive woman.

He went back to staring at St Paul's as Rosalie collected the work contract off his desk. He deliberately didn't make eye contact with her knowing she'd be smiling at him.

He wondered why the name Alex Downton rang a distant bell, but nothing came readily to mind. He was a little concerned that she hadn't given him a lot of information to go on, but he was glad to have the work.

8

CHLOE, CLAUDETTE AND A CALL TO DRURY

After Rosalie returned to the reception area Nick checked his watch and decided it was close enough to lunchtime to grab a bite to eat. Just then, the intercom buzzed.

'Nick, someone else to see you.'

'Okay Rosalie, send them through please.'

His heart jumped and a smile spread across his face as Claudette entered the office. She was as pretty as ever. Her red summer dress was a stark contrast to her strawberry blonde hair and beautiful blue eyes. Nick's mind wandered briefly, the divvy van incident never that far away.

'Well?' she said.

Nick was shocked back to reality.

'Aren't you glad to see me?' Claudette waited for him to respond. When he didn't, she added, 'You did remember we had a lunch date today, didn't you?'

'Yeah, yeah of course!' he lied. 'I was just about to call you!'

'Sure,' she said, knowing full well he'd forgotten all about it.

He got up from his desk, took her hand and squeezed it. As she smiled up at him the same old feelings he had for her came back. He bent forward and kissed her lightly on the lips, then leant over and pressed the intercom button.

'Rosalie, just going to grab an early lunch.'

'Okay Nick,' Rosalie replied. 'Don't forget to say hello to Mr Young and Mr Jackson for me.'

Nick shook his head and grabbed his jacket from the coat rack.

On the way down in the ancient lift Claudette asked, 'So, who was the beautiful woman I saw get out of the lift just before?'

'Just a client.'

'She was very pretty,' she said, then added, 'she totally gave me the evil eye when I got in!'

'Well, her brother— stepbrother,' he corrected himself, 'has gone missing, I guess she's upset.'

Claudette shook her head, not sure how to take that comment.

'So business is good?' she asked.

'Yeah, can't complain.'

'You didn't remember lunch today did you?' Claudette said and gently nudged him.

'Well, it's been a bit busy. You know how it is!'

She grabbed his hand. 'You're still keen for us to go out together aren't you?'

Nick's heart leapt. 'Yes, of course I am! We've made some great memories!'

'What! In the back of a divvy van?' she giggled.

The lift reached the ground floor and he followed her out.

'Well, it *was* memorable!' he laughed.

She looked at him, smiled and linked her arm through his as they walked out into the oven that was Swanston Street.

In the front bar of Young & Jackson the air conditioners were turned up to their maximum but had little effect as the doors to the pub were always kept open. He found a free table and two bar stools.

'Vodka and lemonade?' he asked.

'Yes please,' she said. Claudette sat on the stool. 'So, a drink in the bar before lunch … are we eating down here?'

'No, no. I always have one down here first. I just like to see who's in the place.'

She looked at him and raised her eyebrows. 'Once a cop always a cop, hey?'

He nodded at her with mock seriousness and walked to the bar. The large TV screen overhead caught his attention. A sober-faced newsreader stared out:

The South Australian Weather Bureau has posted
a series of warnings about an enormous storm

*building in the Great Australian Bight. A spokes-
person for the bureau said it is the largest storm
system they have seen for some time and has the
potential to do immense damage. The system has
started to move inland and is travelling eastward
towards Adelaide where they have put out warnings
of damaging winds, flooding and lightning strikes.
Both Mount Gambier and Bordertown have
reported winds in excess of one hundred kilometres
per hour together with soaking rain. The storm is
still building and is likely to sweep across the entire
southern coast of Victoria, with Greater Melbourne
likely to be directly in its path.
We will keep you up to date as more news comes to
hand.*

Nick frowned. He reached into his jacket pocket and
took out the photo of the young man Jessica Downton had
given him. He looked at it again. Alex Downton's face was
somehow familiar, but he still couldn't work out where
from. He put it away and carried the drinks back to Claudette.

'Just got to make a quick phone call,' he said.

'Okay, but don't leave me here all alone for too long.'
She looked around in the bar. 'You never know who might
talk to me!'

'Don't worry, I'll be quick.'

'You said that to me once before!' she said and a broad

smile crossed her face.

Nick smiled back and walked over to a quiet corner. He rang Pete Drury's number.

'Drury!'

'Pete, it's Nick – long time no speak!'

'Nick, good to hear from you. What's up?'

'I was wondering if I could ask a favour?'

'Well,' Drury replied, 'what is it?'

'I was wondering if you could look up an Alex Downton for me. I've got a client who says he is her stepbrother and he's gone missing. His name rings a bell for some reason.'

'Downton, Alex Downton,' Drury repeated.

'Yeah.'

'Okay, but aren't you s'posed to be the private investigator? You know, *you* do the diggin' and brain work, while dumb cops like me run around with our heads up our arse!'

'Yeah, I know, but …'

'Okay, I'll see what I can find on the police database.'

'Thanks Pete, I owe you one.'

'Jesus, Nick. You owe me more than one!' Drury said dryly, 'I'll get back to ya.'

'Thanks Pete,' Nick said and hung up.

Upstairs in Chloe's Brasserie he asked for a table for two. They passed the full-length painting of Chloe, the naked and ageless beauty with her small but alluring bare breasts.

Claudette nodded towards the painting and gently poked him in the ribs. 'Now I know why you always bring me up here to eat!'

'Reminds me of you!' Nick responded and squeezed her hand.

She gently bit her bottom lip and smiled back at him as they followed the waiter to their table.

9

ALEX

Alex was the only child of Helen and came from her marriage to Drew, her first husband. Alex's birth was difficult. Helen spent the last two months of the pregnancy lying in a hospital bed; the doctors said the possibility of losing the baby was too great if she remained upright and mobile.

Alex was born breach and given oxygen as soon as he was delivered. It was touch and go for a couple of days but then he started to gain weight and strength. But it was never easy for him. He was always different. As he got older those differences became more pronounced. He was never outgoing and preferred his own company.

Helen was only sixteen when she married Drew. Their romance started in the workplace. Helen had taken a job working directly for Drew, who was an executive of the company. Drew was divorced and lonely, while Helen was young, beautiful and available. They hit it off from day one and things developed from there. Their obsession with each other really came to a head at a work Christmas party. The alcohol flowed and it was halfway through the night when Drew asked her back to his place. She hesitated for only a moment, then followed him out through a side door, well before the party got into full swing.

They started to see each other regularly, out of work times, and it was only a few months into the relationship that Drew asked Helen to marry him. He knew she was a very young girl, but he didn't care, he wanted to be with her and said he would look after her for the rest of her life.

When Helen told her parents what was happening, and said she was going to marry Drew, they didn't approve. They said she was much too young and she should wait. The talk of marriage was far too premature. But this only added to Helen's determination to be with Drew.

Within the year they were married.

But while she would never admit it out loud, it looked like her parents were right. It was only a few months after Alex was born that the marriage started to break down. Helen found out that Drew suffered from depression. He started drinking, which only worsened his black moods and counteracted any beneficial effects of his antidepressants. As hard as she tried, there was not much she could do but be with him and comfort him. As time wore on they began to argue and Drew became even more distant.

Helen started to spend most of her time with their child, which only upset Drew more. He told her he wished they'd never had the kid and that he had no time for him. Helen was worried for Alex and became fiercely protective of him.

It was Helen who rang the police early on a Sunday morning. She told them she'd found Drew in the garage sitting in his car with the engine running. One end of a plastic hose was attached to the exhaust pipe while the other end had been fed through the driver's side window.

When the detectives arrived, she told them that things had not been good for some time and that Drew had become more and more unhappy as the months went by. She said he'd started drinking heavily and was also using drugs to help fight depression. The autopsy report came back and the coroner confirmed that Drew had both alcohol and a large amount of the antidepressant Trazodone in his system. The finding confirmed Helen's account that Drew had committed suicide and his Death Certificate was marked accordingly.

The payout from Drew's estate was substantial, but not a complete surprise to Helen. She already had joint accounts with him that had plenty of money in them. She also knew he'd seen his solicitor shortly after their marriage and drawn up a new will. Drew told her she was the sole beneficiary. So when the estate was finalised, she received a huge amount of cash, a large portfolio of shares and the keys to Drew's house in Hawthorn.

It was a few years after his death that Helen met and married Victor, who ran a successful manufacturing business. Victor moved into Helen's large house in Hawthorn and brought with him his daughter Jessica, who was in her mid-teens and not that much younger than Helen herself.

When Alex, now four years old, was first introduced to them, he wasn't sure how to react.

'Alex,' his mother said, motioning towards Victor, 'this is Victor.'

'Hello,' Victor said as he bent forward and held out his hand.

Alex just looked at it and didn't move. He was terrified of this tall, strange man.

'And this is Jessica,' his mother continued. 'Say hello, Alex!'

'H-h-hello,' he said to Jessica and a slight smile crossed his face.

Alex stood there for a couple of moments, looking at these strangers in his house, then he turned and ran upstairs to his bedroom.

'He's just tired and a bit shy,' his mother told Victor, making an excuse for his bad manners.

Victor nodded but knew from that moment on he'd never have any time for Alex. The kid was peculiar. He was sure he was disturbed. Helen had told him she had a son, but she never made it known that the kid had problems. He wondered how he would cope with that weird kid in the house.

As Alex got older he found trouble easily. He did things like pulling the tablecloth off the table and sending the dinner plates flying. His bad behaviour just went on and on. One day he broke his mother's best vase. He pushed it off the table next to the front door and it smashed into a thousand pieces.

'Why did you do that?' his mother scolded him after she'd marched him upstairs to his room.

'I ... d-d-didn't do it. It w-w-was the N-Naughty Boy,' Alex said and buried his head in his pillow and began to cry.

'Stop that stuttering,' his stepfather Victor shouted.

He was standing at Alex's bedroom door, as usual, with a stern look on his face; he never went into the boy's bedroom. In fact, he never spent any time with Alex at all.

His mother turned on Victor.

'Don't yell at him! The doctor said it only makes it worse if you yell at him!'

'Well, he's old enough now to stop that stupid talk.'

'He's not stupid!' Helen yelled and tears started to form in her eyes.

'Now tell me, Alex,' she said firmly, 'why did you break my vase?'

'M-M-Mum ... w-when the N-N-Naughty Boy comes, h-h-he takes over. I c-c-can't s-stop him.'

His mother looked down on him with pity. She loved him very much but deep down she wondered why God had given her Alex to look after. It was going to be a lifetime job and she was already so very tired.

'Talk of this Naughty Boy is just rubbish, Helen!' Victor snapped, pointing at Alex. 'It's just him making an excuse for his bad behaviour!'

Helen turned on Victor, her eyes wet with tears. Then she looked back at Alex, put her hand on his forehead and said, 'All right Alex go to sleep now. We can discuss this in the morning.'

She left his bedroom and went downstairs with Victor.

When the coast was clear Jessica came into Alex's bedroom.

'It's okay, Alex,' she said as she brushed his tears away.

'I c-c-can't h-help it!' he stuttered through his sobs.

'I know,' she said and pushed the damp hair off his forehead. 'It's okay Alex. It's okay.'

Alex put his head on Jessica's shoulder. He liked her. She was kind and had a lot of time for him.

Later on that night Alex became restless. He tossed and turned in his bed as his tortured brain began to "switch" and the Naughty Boy came forward again.

'Hey Alex!' the voice inside his head spoke.

'Y-y-yes.'

'That Jessica is nice, isn't she?'

'Y-y-yes. I l-l-like her a l-lot.'

'So do I,' the Naughty Boy said and snickered. 'Have you looked down the front of her tee shirt?'

'N-n-no! Why?'

'Take a look next time. Look at her boobs when she bends forward. You'll like it!'

Alex sat up in his room and stared around in the darkness. He couldn't work out why the Naughty Boy had suggested he look down the front of Jessica's shirt.

But the next day he did, and he had to admit, he liked what he saw very much.

10

THE NAUGHTY BOY

The first time Alex was brought to Aimtree House was after he was convicted for his first really violent crime. Alex told his mother it wasn't him. He said it had been the Naughty Boy again.

Alex was now thirteen, but he still spoke of the Naughty Boy and said it was him who did the bad things. His mother had become used to this explanation for the minor break-ages and general mayhem he caused. Most times she told him it was all right and that the Naughty Boy had better not be naughty again. She hoped that as Alex matured, he would grow out of the Naughty Boy – that it would become a thing of the past. But Victor was not so tolerant. He wanted Alex to stop the nonsense and the stupid reference to the non-existent Naughty Boy.

Victor often scolded Alex and sent him to his room when he misbehaved. From his bedroom Alex could often hear the voices of his mother and stepfather downstairs as they argued. When he couldn't quite make out what they were saying he would get out of bed and put his ear against the bare floorboards of his bedroom. Their voices were a lot clearer then.

But this time it was different. He had been especially bad. Alex lay back on his bed and listened as their raised voices filled the house.

'I don't want them to take him!' his mother yelled. 'Surely we can look after him here. We'll improve the security. We won't let him out of the house!'

'He's gotta go there Helen!' Victor yelled back. 'You've seen what he's done! They can help him. He can't stay here, not after what he's done! It's a court order Helen. He's got to go!'

Alex heard his mother crying. He lay back on his bed and listened. He hated it when she cried.

* * *

A few months earlier

Alex went to a special school twice a week for a half day where he was encouraged to make friends and play outside. But it never worked. He was so different and unpopular that no one wanted to be his friend, so Alex always played alone. But he didn't mind. He preferred to wait until Jessica got home from university and spend time with her. She was kind to him and they would play together in his room for hours.

His mother tried to encourage him a number of times to play outside, just for an hour or so, until Jessica got home.

'Why don't we go outside for a little while, Alex?' his mother asked. 'We could play some games together.'

'I d-d-don't w-want to. I w-want to wait f-f-for J-Jessie to g-get home and p-play in my room.'

His mother was crestfallen at his rejection. She knew he preferred Jessica to her, and it hurt.

It was a few days later that Victor spoke to Helen.

'Jessie tells me you tried to get Alex to play outside in the backyard.'

'Yes, but he doesn't want to.'

'Helen, the boy needs some sun on his body, he looks anaemic! I want you to send him outside for at least one hour every day.'

'How will I do that? He says he doesn't want to.'

'You have to insist, Helen. Don't take any of his nonsense. Just send the boy out there!'

Helen didn't argue. She knew deep down it would be good for Alex to spend some time outside. What she didn't like was the way Victor was always taking control and telling her what to do – with her son!

And so, from then on, Alex was forced to play in the backyard for a couple of hours each day. At first he just sat at the back door and didn't move, but after a week or two he got more adventurous and began to explore the yard. One day he walked over to the fence and noticed that Victor had nailed a trellis to the top of it.

The Naughty Boy came forward and whispered to Alex, 'It's probably there to stop you getting out, you know. But it won't stop me!'

Alex was taller and stronger now. The Naughty Boy grabbed the fence and tested the trellis. He knew if he wanted to, he could pull it down. There was a dog next door and Alex wanted to see it. He could hear the dog digging in the dirt and barking when he got close to the fence. He wanted to pat it. He knew an old lady, Mrs Ashby, lived there. He often heard her telling Scamp to be quiet and stop barking. He never heard a man's voice so he guessed she lived by herself and only had the dog for company.

It was a weekday. Alex heard Scamp pawing at the dirt on the other side of the fence, and occasionally growling and barking. He wondered if one day he would see the dog's head appear under the palings and look up at him from the other side.

He called out to the dog. 'H-h-hello, S-S-Scamp!'

The dog barked again and kept pawing the ground on its side of the fence.

Alex looked back at the house to see if his mother was watching him. He could usually see her through the kitchen window while she was at the kitchen sink, but this time she wasn't there. Maybe she's on the phone, he thought.

When she was talking on the phone, Alex knew she generally sat in the lounge room on the other side of the house. Maybe that's where she was now. He was about to call out to the dog when a voice from deep inside his head spoke. Like always, it stopped him in his tracks. He couldn't do anything else but listen.

It was the Naughty Boy. Alex froze and his facial expression took on a terrified look.

'Hey Alex,' the Naughty Boy hissed, 'you wanna kill the dog?'

Alex started to breathe heavily.

'N-n-no!' Alex said in his mind. 'I l-l-ike the d-dog!'

'You're weak!' the Naughty Boy sneered.

The Naughty Boy checked the kitchen window again, and when he was sure no one was there he got a foothold on the fence and pulled down some of the trellis. He climbed up using the fence rails and peeped over the top. Down below he could see the dog busily digging away.

Alex tried to come forward but the Naughty Boy pushed him back.

'See that spade?' the Naughty Boy said.

Alex could see a spade sticking out of a garden bed in Mrs Ashby's backyard.

'I'm going to get that spade and kill it!'

In the background Alex stammered, 'N-n-no!'

He started to cry but his voice faded away as he felt himself getting weaker and weaker. He was no match for the Naughty Boy.

The Naughty Boy put his leg over the fence, swung the other one over and jumped down into the neighbour's backyard. He walked over to the freshly dug earth and pulled out the spade. The dog was playfully running around his legs sniffing and barking.

'Shut up!' the Naughty Boy yelled.

The dog backed off and barked more aggressively. Now it growled. The Naughty Boy came forward with the spade raised above his head. The dog barked again, this time much louder.

The old lady appeared at the back door.

'Scamp! What are you barking at?' she shouted.

The Naughty Boy walked over to the dog and swung the spade but it dived out of the way. The dog continued to bark. The old lady walked out and into the yard.

'Scamp!' she yelled. 'Stop that barking!'

The Naughty Boy held the spade high again and walked over to her.

'Oh no,' she said in a shaky voice when she saw him. 'What do you want?'

She looked over to Scamp who was cowering in a corner of the garden. The Naughty Boy stepped forward.

'Get out!' she yelled at him. And then, when he didn't move, she said in a frightened voice, 'What … what do you want?'

The old lady was terrified. She put her arms up defensively, but it was no use. The Naughty Boy hit her in the head with the spade and she went down hard, then he hit her twice more until she no longer moved.

The Naughty Boy faded away and Alex turned and walked to where the dog was, calling him.

'H-h-hello S-Scamp.'

The dog hunched down, hearing his soft voice.

'Hello b-b-boy!' he said again and held out his hand.

The dog crawled on its belly over to Alex who started to pat it.

Alex looked down at the blood on his hand and frowned. He wiped it onto the leg of his pants, not sure how it got there. He scanned the backyard and could see the broken trellis on the fence. He looked at the old lady lying motionless near her back porch and had a vague recollection of the Naughty Boy doing something bad to her.

He tried to get back over the fence but couldn't manage it. There was no foothold on this side. Alex stayed in the old lady's backyard for a long time. He could hear his mother calling for him. Eventually he called out to her as he swung the spade back and forth.

'M-M-Mum?'

'Alex! Where are you?'

'O-o-over h-here.'

His mother peered over the fence and screamed when she saw what he'd done.

* * *

The court case in the Children's Court ran for only two days. Fortunately for Alex, Mrs Ashby survived after spending a week in a coma. It was immediately obvious to the magistrate that Alex was not normal and ordered that he undergo tests to determine his mental capability. He appointed a psychiatrist to ascertain what psychological problems Alex faced and asked for a report to be presented to him. He also asked Alex's mother to provide the Court with any medical details and findings she had regarding Alex's condition. After reading the report and associated material he found that Alex should not stand trial for grievous bodily harm by way of 'mental impairment'. He put Alex on a Supervision Order and directed he be sent to a suitable facility for treatment.

Alex was ordered to attend Aimtree House within the week.

11

AIMTREE HOUSE PRIVATE HOSPITAL

It was a Monday morning when the police brought Alex to Aimtree. His mother and stepsister accompanied him. The ride in the police car was an adventure for Alex. They glided along streets he'd never seen before. He was fascinated by the different sights.

Soon they drove through large gates that opened up on either side of a long driveway. White pebbles scrunched under the car's tyres as it headed towards the entrance of a large bluestone building. Alex kept looking to either side, checking to make sure Jessica and his mother were still there. Soon the car slowed to a stop and he held Jessica's hand as he got out.

His mother tried to hold his other hand but he refused and said, 'M-M-Mum, I d-don't wanna s-s-stay here. I w-wanna go home!' Tears started in his eyes.

Helen Downton did her best not to cry and said, 'I know darling, but you have to stay for a little while. They'll make you better!'

They followed the policeman up the wide stairs that led to the entrance of Aimtree House. There was a noisy bustle in there with people moving about and talking. Alex hesitated at the front door.

'C'mon Alex,' Jessica whispered to him. 'We've gotta go in.'

He looked up at her and said, 'O-okay.'

They followed the policeman to the front counter where a sign read:

Reception – Please wait quietly

The constable left when the charge nurse called out Alex's name. Helen Downton stood at the counter and began answering a plethora of questions. During this time Jessica sat with Alex and talked with him, trying to put his mind at ease. Alex looked around at the unfamiliar place. It was huge, cold and frightening.

Alex looked up at Jessica and said, 'J-J-Jessie, I d-don't like it here.' He waited for her to respond, but when she didn't he added, 'I h-hate it!'

Finally, the questions were done and Helen walked over to where they were sitting.

Alex said to her, 'M-Mum, I-I d-d-don't like it h-here. I w-want to g-go home!'

'I know, darling,' she said. 'But you have to stay … for just a little while.' She buried her eyes in her handkerchief. 'I love you, Alex. I'll visit often. I promise.'

Jessica squeezed Alex's hand a little tighter. 'It'll be okay Alex. I'll visit you too.'

Alex smiled at her.

'No need for you to come, Jessica!' Helen glared at her, then snapped, 'I'll be the one to visit Alex!'

Jessica looked at Helen surprised, but didn't speak.

Two nurses who'd been standing in the background walked over to them.

'Hi, I'm Audrey,' a pretty nurse said as she introduced herself. 'We just need to get a quick photo of Alex. We'll give you a copy as well,' she said and smiled at both Helen and Jessica.

The nurse took Alex's hand and tried to lead him to where a camera was set up. Alex baulked.

'I-I w-want Jessie,' he said.

The nurse nodded to Jessica who walked with him to where the photo was to be taken. Alex stood quietly in front of a large oversized print of Aimtree House used as the backdrop. He didn't smile.

'We'll take care of him now,' Nurse Audrey said.

Alex looked at her but remained silent and gripped Jessica's hand even tighter.

'Come on Alex,' Nurse Audrey said as she took his hand. 'You can come with us now. We'll show you your room.'

Helen handed the nurse Alex's duffel bag, which contained his clothes and some toiletries. When Alex saw this he reluctantly let go of Jessica's hand.

'We'll get him settled. You can visit him in a day or two,' the nurse said.

As they led Alex towards the lift he looked back over his shoulder and waved goodbye.

The lift slowly made its way to the third floor where it opened onto a wide corridor. The walls were painted white and overhead lights hummed and shone out brightly as they passed under them. The nurses' shoes squeaked as they walked on the highly polished floor.

Alex noticed numerous closed doors on either side.

'W-w-who's in th-those r-r-rooms?' he asked.

'Other sick people, Alex. We need to look after them as well,' Nurse Audrey said in a soft voice.

'Oh,' he answered.

Just then, an orderly opened a door and a man burst out.

'Arthur!' the orderly called out, 'just wait there!'

A dishevelled man stood in the doorway of his room and stared as they went by. Alex felt the man's eyes on him. He saw his hands twitching – opening and closing. His breathing came in short sharp bursts, then he started to bounce from one leg to the other and screamed and pointed at Alex.

'YOU! YOU!' he cried. He tried to reach Alex but the orderly caught him. The man fought the orderly, still trying desperately to grab Alex.

'Arthur! Settle down! He's new here!' the orderly shouted as he struggled with the man.

Alex backed up against the opposite wall, terrified of the man who continued to stare at him with enormous bulging eyes.

'It's okay, Alex. It's okay. He can't get to you,' Nurse Audrey said and gently nudged him to keep walking.

Alex kept looking back at the man as the nurses took him to his room. Once inside they unpacked his things and showed him around.

'I'll be back a bit later with some warm milk and biscuits. Would you like that?'

'Y-y-yes thanks,' Alex replied in a soft voice.

The nurses smiled at Alex and left the room. He heard the lock click into place as the door was closed. He walked over to the window and stared at the huge pine trees outside as they swayed majestically in the breeze. He wondered why he was here. Had he done something wrong, or had it been the Naughty Boy again, he wondered? He just wasn't sure.

It was later that night, after dinner, that Nurse Audrey came into his room. 'Hi Alex!' she said brightly.

'H-h-hi,' Alex replied.

She placed the milk and biscuits on the table, and as she bent forward he took a quick peek down the front of her shirt. He liked Nurse Audrey. She was pretty and friendly. She was a lot like Jessica.

'Here are some biscuits and milk for you.'

'Th-th-thanks.'

'They'll turn the lights out in about an hour, so make sure you finish this off. I don't want you to miss out. I'll pick up the tray in the morning.'

'O-okay,' Alex said and sat down at the table.

He watched Nurse Audrey leave and listened as the lock on his door clicked. He walked over and grabbed the lock and tried to twist it but it wouldn't budge. He walked back to his bed and got undressed, put on his pyjamas and got into bed. He jumped when the lights were shut off. At first he told himself he wasn't scared, but soon the doubts started to creep in. All night long he heard strange noises and muffled groans and screams coming from the other rooms in the corridor.

He was terrified.

He lay on the bed and began to cry, eventually he fell asleep. In his dream a strange bug-eyed man lunged at him and shouted. He started to chase Alex down a long corridor. Alex ran as fast as he could but he wasn't able to outrun the man with the huge black eyes. Eventually the man caught him, and when he dug his long bony fingers into Alex's shoulder he woke up and screamed and screamed!

12

FIRST MEETING WITH DOCTOR SHELTON

Alex stood in his seclusion room on the third floor of Aimtree House and stared outside. Occasionally he could see birds sitting in the branches of the pine trees. He wondered what it would be like to be out there, instead of where he was now, in this bare room with its plain four walls and high ceiling. What if he could be free, he wondered, just like those birds.

But Alex was looking forward to today. Nurse Audrey had told him he was getting a visitor. She said Dr Shelton was coming to see him and wanted to talk to him. She added that Dr Shelton was a psychiatrist. Alex wondered what a psychiatrist was.

It was two o'clock in the afternoon when there was a knock on the door. He heard the lock click open and through the door came a tall and slender middle-aged man.

He was dressed in a suit and carried a briefcase. He wore wire rim glasses and had a moustache and goatee beard, which were both starting to turn grey.

'Hi Alex,' Dr Shelton said. His moustache and goatee moved up and down slightly as he smiled.

Alex didn't reply. He just stared at this strange new man.

Shelton was interested to understand Alex's psychosis and in particular his reference to the Naughty Boy. He'd never seen a case of dissociative identity disorder, or multiple personality disorder, as it used to be known, and was keen to learn more. To put Alex at ease, he made a point of visiting him in his room, as he believed the familiar surrounds would help make Alex feel safe and perhaps he would talk more freely.

'H-h-hello,' Alex eventually said, as he continued to stare at the stranger.

'My name is Jeffrey,' Shelton explained. 'I'm a doctor – a psychiatrist.'

Again, Alex didn't speak.

'Is it okay if we talk for a while? If I ask you some questions?'

Shelton put his briefcase on the small table, opened it and took out a pad and pen, then sat down.

'O-o-okay,' Alex replied.

'Why don't you sit down?' Dr Shelton said and pointed to the other chair.

Alex pulled it out and sat down.

'So how are you today, Alex?'

Alex hesitated before he answered, 'O-okay.'

'That's good. Is it alright if I ask you about the Naughty Boy?'

Alex nodded.

'So, when the Naughty Boy comes, does he ask permission?'

Alex hesitated, shook his head, then said, 'N-n-n-no, he j-just p-pushes in!'

'Can you stop him?'

This time Alex swung his head from side to side. 'N-n-n-no. H-he's way t-too strong!'

'Where do you go when he comes?'

Alex blinked repeatedly and stared at the floor.

'I g-go into the b-b-background. He p-pushes me down there. It's, it's d-dark. I d-d-don't like it m-m-much!'

'Can you ask him to come forward now?'

Alex looked up with a puzzled expression on his face.

'I-I'll try, but he only c-c-comes w-when he w-w-wants to.'

The room fell silent and Alex closed his eyes. He stayed that way for a few minutes, then he opened his eyes again.

'Well?' asked Shelton.

'H-he's way b-b-back there, but I c-can't m-m-make him c-c-come.'

'Okay Alex, that's okay.'

These sessions went on for months and it was only once that Alex's personality "switched" and a different persona came forward.

His facial expression changed as the new personality

took control and spoke.

'What do you want, fuckhead?' he said.

Shelton was surprised and a shiver ran up his spine as he looked at Alex. There was a look of hatred on the boy's face.

Shelton kept his voice as calm as he could.

'I'd like to know you better, Naughty Boy ... know who you really are and what brings you forward every now and then.'

'Don't call me Naughty Boy. He's gone! I pushed him way back down that black hole. He'll never come back. I'm Tyson. I can beat you up with just one hand!'

Tyson stood and shaped up like a boxer and started shadow boxing.

Shelton was fascinated that in Alex's mind another character had revealed itself.

'No need to beat me up,' Shelton said calmly, 'I just want to talk.'

Shelton leant back just in case. 'I notice you don't stutter.'

'Stuttering is for babies. Only Alex stutters. I'm Tyson, I don't stutter! Even Naughty Boy doesn't stutter, but he's gone to that terrible place, way, way down there, he can't get out – he's stuck!'

'Okay,' Shelton said as calmly as he could. He made a quick note, as he was keen to know more about 'the terrible place', but decided to leave it for now and pursue the bashing of the old lady.

'Tell me, Tyson, why did you hit that old lady, Mrs

Ashby, with the spade?'

Tyson stopped shadow boxing, walked over to the window and stared outside. He didn't speak for a long time. Shelton wondered if he was going to ignore him altogether. Then he turned around and stared at the doctor.

'That wasn't me. That was the Naughty Boy,' he said.

Tyson began breathing heavily. Shelton could tell Tyson was expecting him to challenge him, but he remained passive and didn't respond. Then Tyson rounded on him.

'The bitch deserved it! She yelled at him! I told him no one should yell at him! I didn't like the look of her! He should have hit her harder, really smashed her head in! I should have taken over and got her. Should have got that fuckin' dog too!'

'Are you mad because you didn't hurt her or the dog enough?' Shelton asked.

Tyson glared at Shelton. 'I just told you, it wasn't me!' he shouted. 'I said *I should have taken over*! I should have punched her!' Tyson thrust his clenched fists back and forward again. 'I should have really showed her how hard a fighter can punch!'

'What about the dog?'

'Fuck the dog!' Tyson spat the words out.

'Do you want to hurt anyone else?'

'I only hurt people if they annoy me or get in my face,' he said. 'I don't put up with crap from anyone! Not even you!'

Shelton watched Tyson warily.

'What do you think of Alex? Do you want to hurt him?

'Alex! He's weak – *piss weak*!' Tyson stressed. 'I won't hurt him though, but I like to push him around if he gets in the way! I'm Tyson, I push everyone around!'

He went back to shadow boxing and dancing around the room. Then he stopped and stared at Shelton.

'I'm sick of talkin' with you! You're weak too, just like Alex! You get in my way Shelton and I'll punch your lights out! Piss off!'

The boy began to take short sharp breaths and stood still in the middle of the room. Within seconds his facial expression changed from anger to something bland. He sat down on the floor cross-legged with his head bowed.

'Are you back, Alex?' Shelton asked.

'Y-y-yes,' Alex said in a quiet voice.

'Did you tell the Naughty Boy to go?'

'D-d-don't c-call him N-Naughty Boy, Doctor Shelton. N-Naughty Boy is gone! Tyson p-pushed him a long way down! It's j-just Tyson and m-m-me now. P-please d-don't make T-Tyson angry again. He m-might come back! I d-don't like it w-when he c-c-comes.'

'Okay Alex, okay. But did you tell Tyson to go?'

'N-no, he w-w-went because y-you were m-making him m-mad.'

Alex closed his eyes and his head sunk further into his chest. 'I'm r-r-really t-tired now, D-Doctor Shelton.'

'Okay Alex, we'll call it a day.'

Shelton stood up as Alex lay down on his bed. Alex

turned towards the wall and immediately fell into a deep sleep.

* * *

The file Shelton put together regarding Alex was comprehensive. After a further year of consultations Shelton had finally won Alex's confidence and he got to know him well. He tried many times to get Tyson, or the Naughty Boy, to come back but was never successful. Shelton eventually concluded that the therapy he'd given Alex was complete and that both Tyson and the Naughty Boy had gone forever.

Shelton asked to see Alex's mother and told her he had spoken with the authorities and advised them that Alex had improved sufficiently for him to be allowed back home. But he said he would need constant supervision. He also prescribed heavy medication to help Alex relax. Shelton recommended he be given a light dose of the drug first thing in the morning to keep him calm, a greater dose in the afternoon to help him sleep for about two hours and then a much heavier dose at night, just before he went to bed. He said it would ensure Alex slept the whole night.

Within a month Alex was back at home, and once again it was his mother, Helen, who had the responsibility of looking after him. His stepfather, Victor, was not interested in him at all. His manufacturing business dominated his life.

One night, shortly after dinner, Alex was lying on his bed when he heard his mother and Victor downstairs arguing. He hadn't had his nightly meds yet so he felt alert. He got out of bed and pressed his ear against the bare floorboards like he'd done so many times before.

It was his stepfather who spoke. 'Maybe we should just say he's too much of a handful and send him back to the nut farm!'

'No!' his mother wailed, 'We have to look after him. He's our child!'

'He's your child Helen, not mine. He's just holding us back!'

'Well, we can't just desert him! We have to look after him.'

'Jessica is suffering as well. Her friends have found out she has a brother who's a weirdo,' Victor shouted.

Helen scowled and gritted her teeth at the mention of Jessica.

'He's not a weirdo. He's just a boy who has a mental problem!' Helen yelled back. 'Perhaps if you helped around here a bit more things would be better.'

'I'm helping by keeping the business going. It pays the bills, you know!'

Alex heard his mother walking up the stairs and once again she was crying. He quickly got back into bed.

'W-w-why are you c-c-cryin', Mum?' Alex asked when she came into his room.

'It's nothing, Alex darling. Here take this.' She gave Alex the tablets and he settled back against his pillows. Soon he was in a deep, deep sleep.

13

DOUBLE MURDER

Two years later

Alex got used to the drug routine and was happy because Tyson hadn't visited him for a long, long time. But he knew there was something wrong. His mother and Victor still argued a lot. Once again he overheard his stepfather say he wanted to send him back to the 'nut farm'.

But now there was something else that worried Alex. Jessica had finished university and got a job as a pharmacist. This meant she was regularly home late at night and was often too tired to spend a lot of time with him. Also, he overheard her talking with his mother and Victor one night and telling them she was thinking of moving out sometime soon and getting a place of her own. Alex was devastated when he heard this.

During the days and evenings, it was usually only Alex and his mother who were at home. One afternoon when they were watching TV, he heard the phone ring in the other room. His mother got up straight away and answered it. He noticed she was taking and making a lot more calls lately. This time he decided to eavesdrop. He got up from the couch and snuck to the door where he could listen in.

'Okay,' his mother giggled, 'provided it's no longer than two hours, that's how long he sleeps for in the afternoon.'

When Alex heard her hang up he raced back to the couch and looked at the TV. He was pleased. She seemed happier than she'd been for years. He liked it when she was happy.

Within minutes she said, 'Okay, Alex. Time for your afternoon nap.'

'O-okay M-Mum,' he said and walked up the stairs to his bedroom.

He smiled at her as he lay on his bed, opened his mouth and took the tablet.

'Th-th-thanks, M-Mum.'

She touched his cheek and rubbed his forehead.

'Have a good sleep, Alex darling.'

He closed his eyes, snuggled down in the bed and kept the tablet carefully under his tongue. He waited until he heard her go downstairs, then took it out and put it under his pillow, got up and looked out of his bedroom window. Soon a car pulled up in the driveway. A man got out that Alex didn't recognise. He saw his mother walk over to him and they kissed. Then he watched as the man moved his hand over his mother's bottom. She pushed it away and laughed, then they kissed again. He watched as she led the man back into their house. He heard them talking downstairs and after a couple of minutes they started to walk up the stairs. He got back into bed and pretended to be asleep when his bedroom door was opened slightly and quietly closed again. Then he heard his mother's bedroom door close. He lay there and could hear her laughing, then groaning. He covered his ears with his hands so he couldn't hear the next lot of noises that came from her bedroom.

Alex got used to the man coming to see his mother. He knew it was once a week and always on a Wednesday. Each time he would pretend to be asleep when his mother checked on him. Then he would wait until he heard his mother's bedroom door close before he got out of bed. Initially he would sneak downstairs and watch television, but after a couple of months he got more adventurous and started to leave the house and roam the streets. It was on one of these occasions when he saw a girl across the road. She was standing in her driveway and looked like she was waiting for someone. She was pretty and about the same age as Jessica. She clutched a leather handbag in one hand and a mobile phone in the other. Her high heels were bright red which matched her short skirt. She had long legs and a tight shirt that showed off her small boobs – Alex thought she was a lot like Jessica.

He walked across the road to her.

'H-h-h-hello,' he said.

'Hi,' she replied and smiled. She had no idea who this boy was.

'I-l live j-j-just o-over there,' Alex said and pointed to

his house.

'Oh, that's nice.' She looked towards the large double-storey house.

'Y-y-you're p-pretty,' Alex stammered.

'Thank you.' She looked at him and became a little anxious. She was by herself and this boy seemed strange.

'W-w-what's your n-name?' Alex asked her.

She looked around and hesitated. How could she get out of this and get away from him?

'Sally,' she said reluctantly.

'C-c-can I b-be your b-boyfriend?'

Now she was really worried. She looked at the weird boy and started to feel panicked.

'I'm sorry but I already have a boyfriend,' she blurted out.

Relief washed over her as she spoke the words, she hoped he'd leave her alone once he thought she was spoken for.

Oh,' Alex said with a blank expression on his face.

Without saying another word, he turned and walked away. She shook her head and frowned as she watched him walk across the street to his house.

Each Wednesday when he heard his mother's bedroom door shut Alex got up and looked out of his window. Each time he was looking for her – the girl called Sally! Finally, after a month he saw her again and his heart began to beat wildly. This time she was dressed in tight shorts and an open shirt that just covered her tiny breasts.

But Alex was devastated when a young man arrived in a sports car. He got out and kissed her. Alex was outraged when he saw the boy run his hand over Sally's bottom, just like the strange man had done to his mother. His mind started racing.

This was not right! he thought. *He* was her boyfriend! He'd asked her to be! She was supposed to be with him!

Then he saw something that made his heart sink. He saw her point in the direction of his house and then both her and the boy started to laugh. He was sure they were laughing at him! His world felt as if it was falling apart.

That night, as he lay in bed, Alex told his mother what had happened.

'M-Mum, th-they were l-l-laughing at m-me!'

'They wouldn't be laughing at you, Alex,' she said soothingly. 'They wouldn't even be able to see you through your bedroom window. It's too far away.'

Alex didn't tell her about leaving the house and that he had actually spoken to the girl.

'Y-yes, th-they were, Mum. I s-s-saw them p-point and l-laugh at me!'

Helen scowled. She felt angry and sad that Alex thought people were laughing at him. He had enough on his plate without something like that, but she was convinced it was some sort of coincidence, or maybe just in Alex's imagination. It would be impossible, she thought, for anyone to see Alex through his bedroom window from that distance.

'Okay Alex, well let's forget about them and just go to sleep,' she said and gently tucked him in.

But she also made a mental note of what Alex was saying. She would watch out for the girl, just in case, because no one, *no one at all,* was going to laugh at her boy!

* * *

Tyson lay in wait near to the house where the girl, Sally, lived. Alex was worried that something bad was going to happen as after all this time Tyson had come back, and once again he had been pushed into the background.

Tyson watched as the girl walked out of her driveway and waited by the side of the road for the boy who drove the car.

'They won't laugh anymore!' Tyson whispered to Alex. 'I'll look after that!'

And to make sure they didn't laugh, Tyson had a weapon with him – a large hammer.

'Gonna get 'em good,' Tyson whispered again. 'Really, really good!'

Tyson said to Alex. 'Hey Alex, ya wanna hold it?'

Alex took the hammer. It was heavy. Very, very heavy.

'Feels good, doesn't it?' Tyson hissed. 'Really, really good.'

* * *

The news headlines the next day told of a horrific double murder.

> *There has been a dreadful double murder in the leafy streets of Hawthorn. Two young people are dead. The murderer has used what appears to be a blunt instrument to bash his victims to death, but as yet no weapon has been found. This was a vicious attack that happened in broad daylight. The victims stood little chance. It is believed the boy was killed first followed quickly by the girl. There was a chaotic scene as police arrived. They have apprehended the suspect, who showed no resistance at all when being arrested. This may have been because his mother was first on the scene and had likely calmed him down before the police arrived. The suspect was handcuffed and taken to a local police station for questioning.*

Alex sat in the back seat of the unmarked police car wedged between two burly detectives. He stared out the window and wondered why he was there. His mother followed behind in another police car. Back at the police station it was his mother who answered the questions on Alex's behalf as he was being processed. Afterwards one of the detectives said he wanted to speak to Alex alone and asked her to wait in the cafeteria.

In Interview Room #1 the detective undid the handcuffs on Alex and pointed him to a chair. He was a 'no nonsense' veteran and could tell Alex was different from other people his age. He guessed that he was probably mentally slow.

He waited for Alex to sit down and started to grill him.

'Why did you kill those people, boy?'

'It-it-it wasn't me,' Alex said and stared at this terrifying man.

'Your mother said she saw you with the hammer. You had it in your hand, it must have been you!'

'It-it was … s-s-someone else,' Alex said softly.

'Who?' The detective shouted and leant forward, his face inches from Alex's.

'I-I d-don't w-want to s-say,' Alex almost whispered.

'So, where's the hammer now?'

Tears started in Alex's eyes. But he didn't answer, he just shook his head from side to side and stared down at the table.

The detective asked him a few more questions but Alex had become non-responsive. Eventually he shook his head and gave up. He left Alex alone in the interview room, walked back to the charge counter and completed the arrest warrant and associated paperwork.

* * *

Once again it was an open-and-shut court case. The evidence against Alex was overwhelming. He was charged and convicted of the double murder, but told he would not be required to stand trial on the grounds of being mentally incompetent.

The court again ordered that he be sent to a secure location where he could receive suitable treatment for his psychosis. The prosecution was pleased with the sentence as it meant he would probably be held at a mental institution for the term of his natural life and no longer be a threat to society.

So for the second time in his life Alex was brought to Aimtree House. This time he celebrated his sixteenth birthday in a seclusion room on the third floor. And it wasn't long after he was settled in that the hospital contacted Dr Jeffrey Shelton to ensure he could continue treating Alex's complex psychiatric needs.

14

JEALOUSY AND PLAGIARISM

After a gruelling twelve years of studying for a medical degree from Melbourne University and residencies at various hospitals and psychiatric wards, Dr Jeffrey Shelton finally had the necessary prerequisites to set up his own practice as a qualified psychiatrist.

Shelton was a social climber and desperate to make a name for himself. He mixed only with the right crowd and befriended only those people who he thought could help him get ahead. He joined prestigious organisations such as the Royal College of Psychiatrists and attended every function they held so he could rub shoulders with people of influence. He also met with the president of the National Association of Practising Psychiatrists and invited him to lunch, paying for the bill. During the meal Shelton made sure he mentioned that he had graduated from Melbourne

University and had worked in a number of prominent hospitals and psychiatric wards. He was very keen to be seen in the best light.

Shelton came from a poor family, which was a constant embarrassment to him. As often as he could he would deflect conversations that could potentially lead to someone asking where he was born or where he had lived as a child. During his long years of study his means were meagre and when it came to setting up his practice he called on his parents to see if they could help. His request fell on deaf ears. So Shelton had to settle for a rundown three-bedroom house in Oakleigh, which he converted into his clinic. For the reception area he had a carpenter build a counter at the point where the tiny entrance hall met the lounge. He purchased a desk from a second-hand dealer and put it in the main bedroom, which he used as his consulting room. One other room of the house he used for filing and the rest of the house was shut off.

Despite – or, in some ways, perhaps because of – the working-class aspect of the suburb he was in, he made doubly sure he touched base with the right crowd. He met with the local mayor and the manager of a charity that looked after the homeless and street kids in town. This latter contact, he hoped, might become a ready source of people with depression and similar psychosis. It might also provide a steady stream of paying customers, and give him the opportunity to show off his skill in dealing with people who displayed these conditions.

Shelton tried hard to drum up as many clients as possible, but despite his best efforts over the course of two long and arduous years, he had only managed to see a handful of 'garden variety' patients showing signs of bipolar disorder or schizophrenia. He was, however, successful in gaining a consultancy at Aimtree House, one of the major mental health institutions in Greater Melbourne.

But overall Shelton was disappointed with his lot. He needed to make something spectacular happen; he wanted to be noticed. He was always on the lookout for a break-through patient, a patient where he could show off his skills and impress the mental health hierarchy at large.

Shelton's main rival at university, and the ensuing years of hospital residencies, had been Dr Paul Reading. Reading had graduated from Melbourne University the same year as Shelton and was a top student. He came from a well-con-nected family, was good looking, never without female company – and arrogant to boot. He often got the prime spots in hospitals that Shelton so desired. Shelton tried to connect with him socially but Reading would have none of it. He all but told Shelton he did not associate with people who were clearly inferior to him. The dismissal hurt Shelton badly.

Reading set up his private practice in South Yarra, a most prestigious and desirable location. It took him only a couple of years before he was recognised as one of the leading psychiatrists in Victoria. He always had new ideas and showed brilliant insights concerning how to handle difficult, and sometimes previously untreatable, psychiatric conditions. He wrote numerous papers and had been published in some of the most important medical journals in Australia and internationally.

Shelton was extremely jealous of him. It seemed he would live in Reading's shadow for the rest of his life. Yet the stars aligned for Shelton when he attended a seminar for psychiatrists at the Four Seasons Hotel in Sydney where Reading was the keynote speaker. This, plus the fact that one of his patients, Alex Downton, had been convicted of a double murder and been readmitted to Aimtree House, played directly into Shelton's hands.

* * *

Shelton flew to Sydney on the morning of the seminar and registered early. He spent some time taking in the view of the Harbour, the Bridge and Opera House and in the afternoon he wandered back to the hotel and took a seat at the back of the Grand Ballroom with its plush seats, high ceiling and sparkling chandeliers. From here, he could see who else was arriving and take note of anyone who would be worthwhile meeting. He checked the running sheet. It looked like being a long day; Reading wasn't scheduled to speak until just before dinner that evening.

5:30pm finally arrived and the ballroom was plunged into semi-darkness. The conference chairperson stepped onto the stage and introduced the key note speaker.

'Now ladies and gentlemen, next is the man you have all been waiting to hear from. Please give a generous welcome to one of Australia's leading psychiatrists, Dr Paul Reading.'

Applause erupted as the chairperson moved offstage. Piped music boomed out across the vast room. It seemed to Shelton that a rock star was about to arrive. Soon a figure strode to centre stage. A bright spotlight lit up Dr Reading who was standing facing the audience with his hands raised in the air. The audience continued to clap enthusiastically.

Reading took no notice of them, he simply turned and pointed at the first slide of his presentation as it appeared on the huge screen behind him.

It read:

Electroconvulsive Therapy (ECT) - a cure for
Dissociative Identity Disorder (DID)

There was a collective intake of breath as the audience read the screen. Reading took the microphone.

'Ladies and gentlemen, my name is Dr Paul Reading.'

He paused to let this sink in. Without doubt they knew who he was, but he just loved saying his own name.

'As you all know, DID is a rare condition in which two or more distinct identities, or personality states, are present in, and alternately take control of an individual. Some people describe this as an experience of possession.' He paused, and eyeballed the crowd.

'The person with this condition will also experience

memory loss that is too extensive to be explained by ordinary forgetfulness. You may also know that up until 1994, DID was known as multiple personality disorder.' He reached for a glass of water, took a sip, and then continued.

'DID has many symptoms, such as out-of-body experiences, which sufferers describe as watching a movie of their own self. Common affective states include depression, anxiety, detachment of emotions and suicidal ideation, as well as fantasies of committing violent crime, even as far as murder.'

The audience leant further forward, fully engrossed in what he had to say.

'You may also know that DBS – deep brain stimulation – does not help with this illness. However, ECT has been found to bring about significant improvement in some patients.'

He looked out at the crowd making sure they absorbed his every word.

'ECT is a procedure that in the past has always been performed while the patient was under general anaesthetic.'

There were nods of agreement throughout the audience. Then Reading dropped his bombshell statement.

'Before I go on, my learned friends, I must stress that the procedure I am about to describe has not yet been approved by the Australian Medical Association and has not been tested with full experimental rigour, however I believe it will be accepted in the near future and show to have significant positive effects on patients who were previously thought to be beyond help.'

He paused again, making sure he had their full attention.

'I am recommending that ECT be delivered to patients who are only mildly sedated and therefore awake during the entire procedure!'

The audience gasped.

'In this way, the patient will consciously experience the mild brain seizure produced by the ECT and be aware of how it is affecting their brain.'

Reading went on to explain further benefits of his proposal. People were on the edge of their seats as they listened to what the brilliant young psychiatrist had to say.

Shelton waited for Reading to finish his talk and left while the audience was still applauding loudly. He didn't wait for dinner, even though it brought the possibility of meeting someone influential. Instead, he caught a cab to the airport, booked himself onto the next available flight and went straight back to his Oakleigh practice. This was his chance, he thought!

He was determined to be the first to try the new procedure. He wouldn't wait for approval from the Medical Association; when he proved the procedure was successful, he would be the first to show how it was done. They would follow him and he would get the glory. He would be the one to write the all-important paper and have it published in every medical journal in the country.

With this success not only would he be recognised as a

leading psychiatrist in Australia, he knew that his name –
Dr Jeffrey Shelton – would be known worldwide.

The opportunities from then on would be endless!

15

AIMTREE HOUSE – SECOND STAY

In his seclusion room on the third floor Alex lay on his bed. He recalled the last time he had been at Aimtree. It must have been only a couple of years ago, he thought. Like the last time, the police had brought him here, together with his mother and Jessica, and once again, his stepfather wasn't with them. Even though his mother had asked him to come, Victor had refused. He was always too busy. But it didn't matter to Alex, he hated him anyhow.

As the police car swept into the hospital entrance Alex could see the place hadn't changed at all. The towering building in the middle of the grounds dominated the scene. Alex looked up at the third floor, which no doubt would be his home once more, and checked the barred windows. Each room had a patient staring down at him. A new arrival was one of the only things in the daily routine that broke the boredom. He waved up at them but no one waved back.

They just stared down at him with blank faces. Some comprehended what was going on while others seemed oblivious to their surroundings and the outside world.

The police car stopped out the front of the building. The cop escorted Alex, his mother and Jessica into the reception area. Once again, it was his mother who answered the questions asked by the nurse behind the counter. Alex just stood behind her next to Jessica and listened. He looked around the walls and could see the place was exactly the same. The dark wooden beams were all there as well as the portraits of the old men he didn't know. All of them had serious, unsmiling faces – just like Victor.

The charge nurse finally stopped talking. The policeman smiled at her and said he would leave her to it.

'Hello Alex,' one of the nurses said. 'I'm Desiree, how are you today?'

He never answered as she led him to where his photo was taken once again.

'Back to stay with us. That'll be good!' she said brightly. 'We'll make sure you've got a nice room.'

Nurse Desiree smiled at Alex, his mother and stepsister. 'He'll be okay with us now,' she said.

Helen Downton looked like she was going to cry. 'Goodbye darling.'

But Alex never replied.

Jessica touched his arm and Alex looked at her. 'Bye Alex. We'll come and visit soon.'

'B-b-bye, J-J-Jessie.'

Alex stared long and hard as his mother and Jessica left.

* * *

Alex got up from his bed and walked over to the window. He wasn't happy about being back in Aimtree, but at least this time he had a view. No more boring pine trees, now he overlooked a large car park, which ended with a beautiful grassy square that led to an equally green football oval. In the distance he could see the tops of the tall office buildings that marked the Melbourne CBD.

Nurse Desiree stayed with him for a few minutes and showed him around. Like before, he had a bed, a small table and two chairs. There was a sink and a plastic tumbler where he could get a drink and a cupboard for his clothes. To one side was a small bathroom with a toilet and shower. He waited for her to leave and then walked over to his window. Down below he watched as his mother and Jessica walked to their car and drove away.

He walked back over to his bed, lay down and looked up at the ceiling. He could hear the terrifying, but somehow familiar, screams and shrieks coming from the other rooms. He jammed the pillow hard against his head trying to drown the sounds out.

He tried to recall what had happened, why they had put him here, but he just couldn't remember. He thought it may have been something to do with Tyson, something *he* had done, but he really just didn't know.

16

PREPARATION

A week after Alex had been settled in at Aimtree House, Dr Shelton rang his mother and asked if he could see her.

Helen Downton drove from her Hawthorn mansion, worried about the meeting with Dr Shelton. She wondered what he would have to say. She parked in the car park, checked in at reception and made her way to Dr Shelton's office. She knocked on the door and waited for him to invite her in. She was clearly upset. Her eyes were red from constant tears.

'What happens to my boy now, doctor?' she asked as she stood in the room.

Shelton shifted uncomfortably in his chair.

'Please, Mrs Downton, take a seat.'

He waited for her to sit in the leather visitor's chair.

'Mrs Downton, it is clear to me now that Alex has DID – dissociative identity disorder.'

'What?' Helen Downton sat forward in the chair. 'I thought perhaps he had bipolar, or something similar.'

'I'm sorry, Mrs Downton, but I'm sure that it's much more serious than that.'

Shelton leant back in his chair and let his last statement sink in.

'I have reviewed his case thoroughly and have diagnosed DID. It's a condition in which the sufferer possesses more than one personality. It seems that Alex has one personality that is quiet and somewhat reclusive, this one stutters and is shy. His other personality, however, is almost the complete opposite: this other one doesn't stutter, is outgoing and invariably violent. This personality has the ability to do a lot of harm to people.'

Shelton paused again and waited for a reaction, but she never spoke. He thought that deep down she already suspected this, and had probably done so for a very long time.

'Mrs Downton, I have to ask. Was Alex abused as a child?'

'No! He certainly was not!' she barked at Shelton, but declined to mention that Alex was scared of his stepfather, Victor, who only ever spoke harshly to him.

Shelton waited until she calmed down.

'Mrs Downton, I think I can help Alex – a lot. Indeed, I believe I can cure him.'

He shifted in his chair then went on.

'There is a new procedure available and I would like to try it. I believe it will be very successful and improve his condition significantly.'

Helen wiped her eyes. 'What is this procedure?' Her

tone was somewhat combative.

'It's an electrical process that will stimulate Alex's brain. It will need to be done a number of times, perhaps for twelve months or more, but it will rid him of DID.'

'Will he be allowed to leave here after he's cured?'

Shelton leant back in his chair and considered how to answer this.

'Mrs Downton, the court has directed that Alex be held here indefinitely, or until he is well enough to leave and pose no more threat to the community. What is certain is that if he doesn't receive this procedure, he will never leave this place.'

The tears in her eyes welled up again.

'But I believe I can help him Mrs Downton,' Shelton said with a reassuring smile.

She looked at Shelton and dabbed at her eyes with a handkerchief.

'All right,' she said, as tears rolled down her cheeks, 'but I would like to be there when he gets the procedure.'

Shelton frowned. 'Mrs Downton,' he said, then paused. 'That is not advised. It will look far worse than what it really is for him.'

'I don't care, I want to be there to see what happens, at least a couple of times!'

Shelton looked down at his notes and made a quick entry. Then he looked up at her and smiled.

'Okay, Mrs Downton, as you wish.'

* * *

Six weeks later

Alex lay on his bed as the afternoon light faded and the evening crept in like a thief stealing sunlight. His room became dark, just the way he liked it. He hated it when the nurse put on the light; it reminded him of the procedure.

Oh! The procedure. He didn't like it at all! In his head it was so light – just so, so bright – and the current – oh the current! It hurt so much and made his back ache! But he didn't scream. He wanted to, but as hard as he tried, he – just – couldn't – scream.

Dr Shelton was the one who gave it to him. He used to like Dr Shelton but now he hated him. On one occasion he'd overheard the orderlies talking amongst themselves and one of them said to the other he thought what Shelton was doing to him was illegal.

No wonder it hurts so much, thought Alex, if it's not legal!

He opened his eyes when he heard shoes squeaking on the polished floor as someone walked past his room. He wondered if it was that pretty nurse Desiree. He liked her. She was lovely and had soft hands. Sometimes when she wasn't looking, she'd bend forward and Alex would look down the front of her shirt like the Naughty Boy had told him to do with Jessica all those years ago. She had little boobs, just like the girl who he'd asked to be his girlfriend. He'd liked her too but she was dead now. Maybe Nurse

Desiree would take her place, he thought. Maybe Nurse Desiree would be his girlfriend! Alex smiled to himself as he pondered this thought. He wondered when he might ask her.

He looked over to the door and could tell it was locked by the way the handle twisted upwards. It was locked all right – from the outside! Only Nurse Desiree, Dr Shelton and the orderlies could unlock it. He had tried to open it from the inside on numerous occasions but it was useless. As hard as he twisted the lock, it just wouldn't budge.

He got up and pushed the curtains open so he could see the stars against the night sky. Occasionally, if it was in the right place, he could also see the moon. It was okay when there was only half of it, but sometimes it was full. Alex didn't like it much then; it had a strange effect on him. It messed with his head. When the moon was full, he generally pulled the curtains closed so it didn't shine in his room.

But tonight was okay. Tonight, there were only the stars that twinkled high up in the dark heavens. Alex was anxious, though. The treatment Dr Shelton gave him – the procedure – came around once every two weeks and the next one was due tomorrow morning.

There was a knock on his door. The lock snapped downwards, the door swung open and Nurse Desiree came into his room carrying his dinner.

'Hi Alex,' she said as she put the tray down on his table.

Alex didn't answer. He pretended to be asleep.

'Alex, wake up! Your dinner is here.'

She walked over to his bed, bent over and gently shook his shoulder. Alex opened his eyes and smiled. He also took a brief second to glance down the front of her shirt as it fell slightly open. He looked at the tops of her small breasts then quickly looked away, hoping she didn't see what he was doing.

'Dinner for you!'

'Th-th-thanks,' he said and got up off the bed.

She walked over to the door and turned around.

'Don't forget, I'll be back a bit later on with milk and cookies.'

She looked at him with a worried expression on her face. 'What's wrong Alex? You look anxious.'

'W-w-what time w-will Dr Sh-Shelton b-be here t-t-tomorrow?'

'Oh, about ten o'clock – like always!' she said. 'It takes him a little while to come from Oakleigh during peak hour.' She smiled at Alex.

'I-I don't l-l-like it w-when he g-gets here! I h-hate the p-p-procedure!'

'It'll be okay Alex. It'll be over before you know it.' She smiled sweetly.

'B-b-but I h-hate it!'

'I'll be with you Alex, it'll be okay. I'll stay with you the whole time.'

Nurse Desiree smiled again at Alex and left the room. He heard the lock snap shut. Then he heard her footsteps fade away as she strode down the long corridor.

17

THE PROCEDURE

'This won't hurt a bit Alex,' Nurse Desiree said as she led him into the treatment room.

She helped him onto the special bed, the one with thick leather straps that held him down. Alex didn't like being tied down but he did like Nurse Desiree. He felt her soft, warm breath on his face as she leant over him. He watched as she fixed the straps around his arms and legs.

'This will only last a few minutes, Alex, and then it'll be all over. It's going to help you. It won't hurt a bit!'

'I-I d-don't like it!' he whimpered.

'It'll be okay Alex. It's just a simple process. Remember, it's called ECT.'

'It h-h-hurts!'

'No … you'll be okay. It won't hurt a bit! Not one little bit!' she repeated and patted his hand as she smiled down at him.

He flinched as the sharp prick of the needle entered his arm; within seconds he felt the mild anaesthetic kick in and his body began to relax. He took a quick look around the room before Nurse Desiree finished tying his head down. He looked out through the large windows. He saw his mother there – watching!

Dr Shelton entered the room and, despite the effects of the anaesthetic, Alex began to panic. He squirmed under the straps. His chest heaved up and down as he sucked in the cold, sterile air. His heart thumped as Dr Shelton got closer.

'Hi Alex! This will all be over in no time. Won't hurt a bit!'

Tears formed in Alex's eyes as Dr Shelton busied himself with the electrodes.

A voice boomed out from speakers overhead, 'Hold still. Do not move.'

Alex tried to wriggle but it was impossible.

Dr Shelton bent over him and said, 'Okay Alex, keep calm and make sure you keep your head very still.'

'Just relax Alex,' Nurse Desiree repeated and smiled.

His eyes darted from one side to the other. He couldn't move his head if he wanted to, it was strapped down so tight. He was so constricted that he couldn't move his body at all. He could see the room had a whole wall of windows with doctors in white coats peering in.

But he wanted out! He didn't want any of this! He – just – wanted – out!

'Only a couple of minutes, Alex. It won't hurt a bit, not one little bit!' Nurse Desiree repeated and gently tapped his hand as Dr Shelton placed the cold electrodes on either side of his head.

His breathing came in short, sharp bursts, and like always he closed his eyes tight. In his mind it was dark, as though he were in a tunnel, a long dark tunnel that was large and square. It was either metal or concrete, he couldn't tell. And there was a light way down the end, a tiny square of light. He concentrated on it and waited. All of a sudden, his vision lit up as if a thousand floodlights had all been switched on at once. It filled his head as the electricity surged through his brain. He wanted to scream but nothing came out. His back lifted off the bed as far as the straps would allow as his muscles contracted. His eyes sprung open and he could see the dull white ceiling. He moved his eyes from side to side and saw Nurse Desiree. She wasn't smiling. She looked worried. The electricity subsided momentarily, then, like a thousand bees all stinging the inside of his head at the same time, it came back again, twice as bad! It felt like his skull was being torn apart.

He tried to scream and tell them to stop! Please stop! Please stop! Stop! Stop! Stop!

His back ached as it arched again involuntarily. The lights in his head were at full luminance. It was blindingly bright! He thought he could see inside his own brain: every neuron, every cell, every connection. It was just so, so bright!

'Won't hurt a bit! Not one little bit!' he could hear Nurse Desiree saying over and over again.

'Bullshit! Bullshit!' he wanted to scream but nothing came out. 'Stop it – pleeeeaaaase – you're killing me!'

And then just before it finished, he experienced the final humiliation. He felt a warm and wet sensation in his track-suit pants. He'd pissed himself – in front of pretty Nurse Desiree, he'd pissed himself. Tears filled his eyes.

'It's okay, Alex. We'll fix that,' she said and smiled. 'It's all over now,' she said and began untying the straps holding him down. 'We'll fix all of that right up!'

After the third of the treatments, his mother came into Alex's seclusion room to see him.

'Hello Alex darling, how are you going?'

'M-M-Mum I h-hate it here. I-I w-want to g-go home!'

'I know darling, but you have to stay—'

'I-I-I don't want to! It h-hurts my head! It-it h-hurts e-e-everything!' Alex said and started to cry.

Helen put a hand on her son's shoulder. She wanted to cry as well.

'I c-c-can't tell them t-t-to stop. M-m-my voice d-d-doesn't work. I w-want t-to tell them, to st-st-stop! Stop! Stop! But I c-c-can't!' Alex sobbed.

'I'm sorry Alex, but it's best for you. Dr Shelton says it will make you better.'

Alex's tears continued as his mother sat down next to him and put her arm around him.

Then she saw Alex's face change. He stopped crying and became angry. He stood up and pushed over the small table, sending it flying. He picked up a chair and threw it at the wall. A low guttural noise came from deep inside his throat.

'Alex you mustn't—' his mother stopped talking when she heard her son's voice.

'Get out!' Tyson screamed. 'Get out before I kill you! Get out!'

Helen backed away towards the door. She couldn't believe what she was seeing. An orderly burst through the door.

'Are you okay, ma'am?'

'Yes, yes, I just think Alex needs some rest.' She backed off further, but this time she was really scared.

Tyson stepped forward. The orderly grabbed him and they struggled.

'Fuck off!' Tyson screamed at him. 'Fuck off or I'll kill you!'

But the orderly was strong and used to handling patients in these sorts of situations. He held Tyson by the arms and forced him to sit on the bed. Tyson tried to break his grip but the orderly was too strong. Eventually he stopped struggling and Tyson faded.

Alex sat on the bed with the orderly still holding him. His head dropped to his chest. The orderly let him go and Alex lay down.

'I think he's okay now,' the orderly said to Helen.

'Did he hurt you?' she asked.

'No. It looks like he just wants to sleep.'

The orderly picked up the table and chair, then ushered Helen out of the room. Alex heard the lock click shut.

Tyson came forward again. 'You're weak Alex! You pissed yourself!'

In the background Alex replied, 'I know, I-I c-couldn't help it. It-it hurt so m-m-much!'

'Don't worry, I'll take over from now on. You can hide in the background. They won't hurt me with that fucking procedure! I'm Tyson!'

Alex felt Tyson fade again. He was terrified each time Tyson came forward, but was glad this time. He was very happy that it would be Tyson who got the procedure from now on and not him.

Back in his office Dr Shelton heard what had happened in Alex's room and asked to see his mother before she left.

'Mrs Downton, you've seen a few treatments now and I believe it would be better if you didn't see Alex for a while.'

'What do you mean?' she said and sat down in the visitor's chair.

'Alex is in a very fragile state of mind at the moment, and particularly so after he receives the procedure.'

'But he's my son!' she demanded.

'You've seen how he has reacted, and it could get worse before it gets better. I'm sorry, but I have to restrict your access for the next six months. His mind needs time to heal. Six months from now he will be a lot better and you can continue to see him again, as regularly as you wish.' Shelton looked down at his desk, leant back in his chair and added, 'It's what's best for him.'

'He told me the procedure hurts him doctor!'

'It's only very short-lived, Mrs Downton. He will be much better after a while.'

She remained silent for a moment then said, 'He'll be frightened here by himself. There's no one here he knows.'

'Oh, but there is someone, Mrs Downton – someone he likes very much!'

She looked quizzically at Shelton. 'Who?' she asked forcefully.

'Alex likes Nurse Desiree Thompson very much. He likes her and trusts her.'

'Why does he like *her* so much?' she demanded.

Shelton paused. 'Well, it's a bit delicate, but he says he likes her because she's pretty and … he likes her small breasts. She reminds him of a girlfriend he once had.'

Shelton let his final comment sink in. 'I think he's attracted to her. He's starting to mature sexually, you know.'

'He's never had a girlfriend,' said Helen. 'Only some girl who laughed at him!' She glared at the doctor, stood up and left his office without saying another word.

* * *

Alex got up from his bed and peered down into the hospital car park. He saw his mother leave. Then a little while later he watched as Dr Shelton left for the day. He saw him get into his black Mercedes Benz convertible. He knew the car well. He checked for it every morning and dreaded when he saw it pull up in the car park. That meant he could be getting the procedure again.

He walked over to the door in his room and tried to open it, tried to get away, but as always it was securely locked.

18

ESCAPE FROM AIMTREE HOUSE

Tyson endured another year of the procedure. His back arched as every muscle in his body contracted, but he didn't try to scream. Tyson looked at the pretty nurse with eyes full of hate. The bitch said it wouldn't hurt! What a load of crap! It hurt all right, but Tyson wasn't going to tell anyone. He hated Nurse Desiree, but not as much as he hated Dr Shelton. He hated Dr Shelton much, much more.

It was eight o'clock in the evening and Alex waited for Nurse Desiree to bring supper: cold milk and two biscuits. Evenings were a lot quieter as most of the staff had left for the day, leaving only a small critical team on duty.

He lay on his bed and heard the sound of shoes squeaking as they came down the corridor and stopped in front of his door. Anticipation built in his body like a sprinter waiting for the starting gun. He heard the lock click open and watched as Nurse Desiree walked into the room holding a small tray.

'Hi Alex,' she sang out sweetly and smiled at him.

Alex got up from the bed and walked over to the table where she put the tray down. He felt Tyson with him and tried to push him into the background.

'N-n-no!' he said out loud as he felt himself being overpowered. He looked at Nurse Desiree pleading with her to get out of the room.

'What, Alex?' she asked. 'What did you say?' She looked at him quizzically.

Then Tyson fully emerged and shoved Alex down that terrible dark black hole. His deep voice boomed out.

'Give me the key!' he demanded.

Nurse Desiree looked startled. She noticed that Alex's face had changed and immediately realised she was in danger. She started for the door but Tyson grabbed her and covered her mouth with his hand. She tried to scream but it was muffled. She had no chance to alert the orderly who regularly walked the corridors. Tyson forced her on the bed. She kicked and punched but it had little effect. She was no match for him.

Tyson had planned what he was going to do for a long time now. He grabbed pieces of clothing he'd cut up over the last few days from under his pillow and stuffed some of them into her mouth. She struggled and gagged but he held her down. He took a long piece of cloth, put it around her mouth and tied it at the back of her head. He grabbed her wrists and tied them behind her back. He bound her feet together and secured them to the foot of the bed. For good measure, he looped a noose around her neck and attached it to the bars of the bedhead. He stood up, satisfied with his work, seeing she could hardly move at all.

'See how you like being strapped down, bitch!' he shouted.

He lifted her shirt and peeked down at her boobs for a brief moment then he went through her pockets and found the key to the door. It was the only one there so he hoped that it would unlock any other door that might be in his way when he tried to get out. Before he left he looked down at her once more. He hated her. He wanted to hurt her and hear her cry out in pain, but that would have to wait. Right now, he needed to get away.

He opened the door and took a brief look outside. There was no sign of the orderly. He quickly left the room and locked it. He strode down the corridor checking every door he passed hoping that each one was locked and that no one would suddenly appear. At the end of the corridor, he saw the buttons for the lift, he walked over and hit the 'down' button. There was a mechanical clang as the lift engaged and started to make its way up the shaft. A small bell chimed as it reached the third floor and the doors slid open; there was no one inside. He got in and pressed the button for the ground floor. The doors slid closed. He watched the floor indicator as the lift slowly descended. It stopped with a jolt at the second floor. The doors opened and a nurse walked in. She looked inquisitively at Alex and knew him straight away.

'Hello Alex,' she said and smiled. Then she frowned, as she saw he was there by himself. 'What are you doing out of your room?'

When he didn't reply she knew there was something wrong. She was about to get out when Tyson grabbed her. He put his hand over her mouth and pulled her close to him. He punched the ground floor button again. She kicked and struggled but Tyson hung on tight. The doors closed and the lift slowly continued its downward journey.

Now here's a problem! Tyson thought. What do I do with the nurse?

When the lift reached the reception area he peered around and saw it was empty. The nurse struggled and managed to push his hand away from her mouth.

'Help!' she yelled before he covered her mouth again.

She bit one of his fingers and he pulled his hand away instinctively.

'Alex!' she said trying to reason with him. 'Don't hurt me. Please! Let's go back to your room.'

'Noooo!' Tyson screamed.

She tried to get away but he grabbed her again and dragged her to the front door. He tried to open it, but it wouldn't budge.

'Unlock the door!' Tyson yelled at her.

'I can't, Alex! It's controlled from the security area!' she gasped and frantically looked around to see if anyone was there who could help.

Tyson remembered the key he'd taken from Nurse Desiree. He put it in the lock and twisted it, but nothing happened. A twinge of fear raced through his body. He tried again but the lock held shut. He started to panic but told himself he was Tyson and Tyson never panics. What he needed was a new plan.

He pushed the nurse to the ground, then grabbed a table and dragged it underneath a window. He looked around and picked up a wooden chair from the waiting area. It would make a lot of noise but he didn't care. He had to get out. He took a mighty swing and threw the chair through the window. The glass shattered and spilt out onto the path outside. He pushed the remaining glass out of the window frame with his bare hands, chanced a look back and saw that the nurse was on a phone calling someone.

He climbed out, cutting himself on one of the glass shards and leapt onto the path below. He heard voices coming from inside - male voices! He got up and ran across the front of the bluestone building and around to the back of the hospital. The voices followed him.

'Maybe he's 'round here!' someone shouted. 'Quickly, quickly!'

Tyson sprinted across the grounds and over to the tall cyclone wire fence. He began to climb. The wire mesh clinked and jangled as he dug his fingers in and forced his way up.

'Over here – I can see him!' another voice yelled.

He glanced behind and saw two orderlies running as he got to the top of the fence.

'There he is! Quick! Quick!'

Tyson didn't wait any longer. He scaled halfway down the other side of the fence and jumped the rest of the way. He tumbled to the ground, got up and started to run into the hot summer's night. He ran down street after street, turning corners wherever he could, trying to make sure they couldn't follow him.

He ran until he was exhausted. Finally, he had to walk. He sucked in great lungfuls of the warm night air as he wandered down unfamiliar streets and passed dark houses. As he slowed down Tyson faded into the background and Alex came forward. He checked out the small cuts on his fingers and the larger cut on his arm. For a while he wondered where he was and what had happened, but like watching a movie of himself, slowly parts of his memory started to come back. He recalled bits and pieces of running and climbing. But whatever had happened he knew he was out of Aimtree House.

He was sure that it must have been Tyson who had helped him escape. But he didn't care. Now, at last, he was free and he hoped that he was never going back!

19

ANGIE AND LIAM

At mid-morning, Nick's intercom buzzed.

'Yes, Rosalie?'

'Nick,' Rosalie half whispered, 'Angie's here to see you.'

Nick's stomach dropped. He could see his ex-wife through the glass partition of the door. She had her hand on her hip and a nasty look on her face. He couldn't see Liam.

'Is Liam with her?' he asked Rosalie.

But before Rosalie could answer, Angie, dressed in smart city clothes, marched through the door to Nick's office followed by their son.

'Hi,' Nick said and waited with trepidation for the caustic response that was no doubt coming.

He wasn't disappointed.

'Can you look after Liam?' she asked. 'I'm going shopping!'

'Sure. No worries. How long are you going to be?'

'As long as it takes!' she snapped. 'You'll need to get him

lunch as well.'

'All right, all right. Certainly. No problem.'

'Don't buy him takeaway either. Get him something healthy, like a salad roll. Rye bread. And no soft drink! Only water.'

'Okay, will do!' Nick felt like he was in a boxing match waiting for the knockout blow.

Then she turned to the boy. 'I'll be back in a couple of hours, Liam. Your father will look after you while I'm away.'

Liam half smiled at his mother, then looked across anxiously at Nick. Angie stared at Nick for a moment, then turned and walked out through the reception area and over to the lift.

'Hi Li,' Nick said and smiled.

'Hi Nick,' Liam replied.

'You can call me Dad, like you always do!' Nick said.

'I'm not allowed to anymore,' Liam replied.

'What do you mean you're not allowed to?'

'Mum says I have to call Kelvin Dad from now on.'

'Kelvin! Who the f …! Who is Kelvin?'

'Mum's new boyfriend. He's going to move in, Mum says.'

Liam walked over to the basketball ring, picked up a paper ball and threw it at the backboard.

'How long has your mother been seeing Kelvin?'

'Dunno,' Liam shrugged his shoulders and picked up another paper ball. 'He buys me stuff though.'

'Like what?'

'Like toys. You know, educational toys. Mum says you're hopeless at that.'

Nick shook his head and briefly stared out the window. Liam threw another paper ball at the ring.

'Mum says you were hopeless at most things,' Liam said as he reached up and bent the ring down so he could push a ball through.

Nick took a deep breath and changed the subject.

'Hey, you wanna catch a movie while Mum's shopping?'

'Yeah, but it depends,' Liam said.

'Depends on what?'

'It's gotta be educational, like. Mum only lets me see educational stuff.'

Nick pondered this for a moment, then said, 'Okay, I've had another thought. You wanna play pinball?'

'What's pinball?'

Nick felt like he was one hundred years old.

'Never mind. You wanna drive fast cars?'

'Yeah, okay, but I'm too young to drive cars.'

'No worries, these ones are on a screen. It's really cool. And we can get lunch while we're out.'

Liam looked up at his father.

Nick went on. 'You like hamburgers?'

'I'm not supposed to have them.'

'You like hot chips, Coke, ice cream?'

'Yeah, but mum says I can't have any.'

'No worries. We won't tell her.'

Liam looked at Nick, pleased and worried at the same time.

The walk to Pinball Heaven took about ten minutes. Nick and Liam drove the fast cars, played air hockey and tried their luck shooting hoops. Lunchtime came and Nick ordered burgers, chips and Coke. Liam loved it. He also threw up on the way back to Nick's office and by the time they made it to the sixth floor Liam was *green*.

Rosalie took one look at the young boy and said, 'You want me to look after him for a bit?'

'Yes please, Rosalie!' Nick said and gritted his teeth.

Angie arrived a bit after two o'clock. By this time Rosalie had cleaned Liam up and given him lots of water. Nick thought he looked all right.

Angie stared at her son with concern. 'What's the matter, Liam?'

'I don't feel so good,' Liam moaned as he squirmed in the visitor's chair.

'Why, what's wrong?' Angie asked him.

Liam rubbed his tummy. Nick waited for Liam to answer and grimaced knowing what would follow.

'I think it might have been the rye bread,' he said. 'The crust was really tough.'

Nick's eyes opened wide. Angie crossed her arms and stared at them both suspiciously, but didn't speak. Nick looked at Angie and raised the palms of his hands as if to say, *I did my best!* He couldn't believe what he'd just heard Liam say.

He smiled at her and said, 'I think he'll be all right.'

When Angie looked away he winked at Liam who winked back. Deep down he was convinced his son was a chip off the old block – even if that block was a little rough around the edges.

* * *

Two hours later

Nick was on his mobile when he saw the red light blink on the office phone. He finished his call just as Rosalie buzzed the intercom.

'Nick.'

'Yeah?'

'It's Angie on Line 1.'

'Oh thanks,' he said in a downtrodden voice, not wanting to deal with her again.

He hit the button on the telepad, 'Yes, Angie?'

His stomach felt like lead. Perhaps Liam had fessed up after all. Maybe she'd given him the third degree, or tortured him to find out why he'd been sick.

Before she could speak he said, 'Why don't you take my mobile number?'

'I don't know it and I don't want it!' she replied angrily.

'Just take it, please! You know, if there's an emergency.'

He read out the number before she could respond and heard her tapping the digits into her phone.

'You got it?'

'Yes!' she half shouted.

He could hear her breathing deeply, trying to compose herself.

'Have you been following me?' her voice got louder as she spoke.

'No,' Nick replied, surprised.

There was a pause.

'Well, someone has! I saw them twice in the rear-view mirror on the way home and then again as we got out of the car!'

Another pause.

'There's no need to have me followed Nick. You know where we live!' She was really angry now.

'I didn't!'

'Just stop it!'

'Angie, I swear I—.' The line went dead as she hung up.

Nick replaced the phone in the cradle, swung around in his chair and stared out the office window.

He was worried. This was strange. Who could possibly be following them?

20

LUNCH WITH PETE DRURY

The front bar of Young & Jackson was packed. Outside it was close to forty degrees. Inside it wasn't much better. Detective Pete Drury stood sweating directly under one of the pub's battling air conditioners and waited for Nick to turn up.

It was lunchtime and the place was buzzing. The bar was packed with drinkers; the pub was selling beer as though every pot came with a ticket to the lottery. Soon Nick entered the bar. Drury spotted him and waved. Nick shouldered his way through the crowd and leant on the high round table Drury had managed to commandeer.

'Thanks for coming, Pete!' Nick said and wiped the sweat from his forehead.

'No worries, mate.' Drury smiled. 'By my reckoning, it's your buy!'

Nick looked at Drury and was about to protest, then thought better of it. He fought his way to the bar and brought back two pots of Carlton Draught.

'So, Pete,' Nick said as he took a sip, 'find out anything?'

'Interesting bloke your Alex Downton,' Drury said as he picked up his pot. 'Done two stints in Aimtree!' Drury swallowed half of the pot in one gulp and squinted as the icy cold beer raced down his throat.

'Aimtree?' Nick asked.

'Yeah, you know, Aimtree House, the loony bin on the other side of the river.'

'Oh yeah,' Nick said as he nodded his head and looked into the distance.

It jogged Nick's memory, reminding him of the photo Jessica Downton had shown him. The building in the background could have been Aimtree.

'Both times were court orders. One for bashing an old lady, Thelma Ashby, senseless.'

Nick's memory was coming back. He wondered if that was where he'd heard Downton's name before.

'The second was for a double murder!'

'What? Double murder?' Nick asked incredulously.

'Yeah! Young couple bashed to death with a hammer, just across the road from where Downton lived.'

Drury took another mouthful.

'Blood everywhere. We found him in the driveway of the young female victim's house. Downton's mother found him first. Said she'd seen what had happened from across the street. She calmed him down before we turned up.'

Drury paused and looked around the bar checking out the patronage.

'Ritzy suburb, big two-storey houses and beautiful gardens,' Drury remarked then belched loudly.

Two men walked past and Drury watched them as they made their way to the bar. Eventually he turned back and faced Nick.

'Was no problem arresting him, he just stood there lookin' lost! His mother came with him to the station. She was pretty distraught. Him though ...' Drury shook his head and took another sip, 'he just sat there and said he didn't do it.' Drury looked at Nick and tapped his temple a couple of times. 'Fucked in the head, mate. Kid's a dead-set nut case!'

Nick took a long draw on his pot.

'Gets better though!' Drury added.

Nicked looked at Drury and frowned, 'How?'

'Found out Downton escaped from Aimtree a few days ago. They still haven't found him.'

Nick's frown got deeper.

'How come I never heard about it? I didn't see anything on the news.'

'Aimtree people told us they wanted to keep it quiet – reckoned they'd find him next day. Guess what, they didn't! Prick's still out there somewhere.' Drury jabbed his thumb in the general direction of the outside world.

Nick's mind started to work overtime.

'Did you check his mother's place?'

'Yeah,' Drury said disdainfully. 'Us cops aren't totally dumb, you know!' He paused. 'There was no one at the house when we called. Put surveillance on it for a couple of days but no one turned up. Eventually that team got called away. But we'll still keep checking every now and then. His mother's gotta turn up soon.'

Drury drank the rest of the pot in one gulp. 'Funny thing, though, there's no sign of her husband either – the kid's stepfather,' he added as an afterthought. 'It's like they've both just disappeared!'

Drury looked around the bar checking out who else was there. 'When you rang you said his sister was looking for him.'

'Yeah, that's right,' Nick replied, then added, 'his step-sister, actually.'

Drury nodded. 'So?'

'So what, Pete?'

'So, give me the rundown. Where does she live?'

'I'm not sure. I didn't get her address.'

'Some private detective!'

'Well, she left before I could get it! I've got her mobile number though.'

Nick looked up the contacts on his phone. 'Here it is.'

'Text it to me, okay? I'm hungry, and if I remember rightly, it's your turn to buy lunch as well!'

Nick shook his head and led the way upstairs to Chloe's Brasserie. He asked for a table for two and they waited while the waiter checked the bookings.

Nick looked over to Drury. 'Jesus, I thought this was just a simple case of a missing person,' he said and rubbed his forehead. 'She said he was supposed to be staying with her.'

'Maybe he is with her! We keep an eye on her and we might find him,' Drury added and shrugged his shoulders.

'Hang on, mate, this is my investigation. I'll find him and I'll bring him to you.'

'He's escaped from a mental institution. He's a convicted murderer. It's a cop matter!' Drury eyed Nick.

'Give me a break, Pete! I'm not exactly flush with cash at the moment. I need to find him and get paid.' Nick was desperately hoping Drury would agree. 'When I get him, I'll contact you and make sure you're the arresting officer. It'll look good on your record.'

Drury considered this for a moment and then nodded. 'Okay, but no promises. There's already a couple of cops who've contacted the Aimtree House geniuses. They're workin' pretty much in the background at the moment, letting Aimtree do the hunting. They reckon he won't get far. Besides, if Aimtree find him it'll show just how responsible they are!' Drury laughed harshly. 'Okay, mate. I'll give you a few days grace. Don't mention this to anybody though – if the brass finds out it'll be the end of my brilliant career.' Drury hesitated, then added, 'If you or the Aimtree people haven't got him by the weekend, we're comin' in,' he paused for dramatic effect, 'with the full force of the law.'

'Thanks, mate,' Nick said as they followed the waiter to a table.

As Drury sat down he added, 'Another interesting fact: you know that murder in South Melbourne we were at, you know, you and that young chick,' Drury looked at the ceiling trying to recall her name, 'in the divvy van! You remember!'

'Of course I bloody remember!' Nick said and gave Drury a look of contempt. 'It's Claudette! Why are you bringin' that up?'

'Okay, okay,' Drury said trying to calm Nick down. 'The girl murdered in the house was Audrey Withers, a nurse at Aimtree. Apparently she looked after Downton when he was there during his first incarceration.'

'Jesus!' Nick murmured.

'Yeah, she was also bashed to death with a blunt instrument – same MO as the double murder. There's a good chance it was him after he got out the first time.'

Nick shook his head. The information Drury had was becoming overwhelming. He sat there trying to piece all of it together.

'Okay, snap out of it!' Drury remarked. Then he turned to the waiter who was hovering at the table.

'I'll have the porterhouse thanks, mate. Medium rare. And some seeded mustard on the side.'

'Oh yeah, same for me,' said Nick. 'And bring a bottle of house shiraz, please.'

Drury waited until the waiter left and then bent forward

and lowered his voice.

'House shiraz? All that valuable information I give you, and you order the *house shiraz*?'

'Fair go, mate! I'm a struggling Private D!' Nick replied and finished his pot.

21

THE DOWNTON HOUSE

At lunchtime the following day, Nick was back in the front bar of Young & Jackson when he took a call from Rosalie.

'Nick, Jessica Downton's here to see you.'

'Oh … really?'

'And Nick, I'm a bit worried.'

'What, why?'

'I've had some weird email messages come through. They're a bit scary!'

'You've been doin' too much online shopping, Rosalie. You probably just clicked on a bad site.'

'No Nick, they're not directed to me. They're all for you. I've been checking your inbox while you've been gone. The messages are all sent to you!'

He got up from his bar stool and shook his head, wondering how Rosalie had got access to his computer. No doubt he'd left his password in the open somewhere or jotted it down absentmindedly. He was about to leave when a news flash spread across the half-dozen large TV screens mounted overhead around the bar.

Breaking News –
The border towns of Mount Gambier and Penola near the South Australian border, together with Edenhope, Casterton and Horsham on the Victorian side have all reported torrential rain and gale-force winds. The storm front that originated in the Great Australian Bight has started to move inland. The damage so far is substantial with many houses suffering significant wind damage. Others have been inundated with floodwaters and several have been completely washed away.

People everywhere in the Victorian Western District are advised to prepare for very strong winds, flash flooding and the potential for numerous lightning strikes. So far this weather pattern is moving very slowly, which has only added to the devastation recorded in these tiny border towns.

The weather bureau has advised there is a very real chance that the storm will strike Melbourne in the next couple of days. We will keep you informed as more information becomes available.

Nick walked out into the oven that was Swanston Street. The direct rays of the sun were so hot it felt like his hair would catch on fire. He looked up. The sky was an eerie whitish-grey colour. The clouds scudded by at an incredible pace.

He rode the metal lift up to the sixth floor and walked into the reception area.

'She's in there, Nick,' Rosalie said, pointing to his office. 'And Nick, she's hot – I mean really, really hot!'

'Rosalie!' Nick said and frowned at her.

She pulled a face.

Nick walked into his office and saw Jessica sitting in the visitor's chair. She got up as he walked in.

'Hello Miss Downton,' he said.

'Mr Jarratt,' she replied as Nick walked over and sat down behind his desk.

She had on tight silk shorts, long white boots and a dark green shirt unbuttoned so it showed more than a hint of cleavage.

Rosalie was right, Nick thought. She's smokin'!

'That week's come around quick,' he quipped.

'I know I'm a bit early, but I wondered if you had found Alex, or had any information as to where he might be.'

She clutched her handbag. Nick noticed the thin white gloves once again draped over the clasp.

'No, nothing yet. But I do have a few leads – nothing solid, though. Not yet, anyhow. Please Miss Downton, take a seat.'

'You can call me Jessica, Mr Jarratt, I don't bite.'

Nick was taken aback for a moment. He was about to concede to her that she could call him Nick, but he hesitated; he wanted to keep this, as best he could, on a professional level. Instead he smiled and watched as she sat down. He couldn't take his eyes off her.

'Okay … Jessica. By the way, where do you live? I didn't get your address last time.'

'Why do you need it?' She became defensive.

'Perhaps Alex will come back. And if you don't mind I'd like to have a look around just so I understand the landscape.' Nick smiled, hoping it would win her confidence.

* * *

They drove out of the CBD in her green E-type Jaguar and over to her mansion in Hawthorn. It was a spectacular neighbourhood. The street was full of beautiful two-storey houses with immaculate gardens. Nick couldn't help but be impressed.

'Well, here we are Mr Jarratt,' she said and climbed out of the driver's seat.

He got out and couldn't help but take a quick glimpse of her tight bottom as she walked through the front gate and up the pathway bordered by a beautifully manicured lawn.

Nick remembered pictures of this place from TV news footage. 'Isn't it somewhere around here that a double murder took place?' he asked.

'Yes, it is. Just over there,' she said and pointed to the driveway of a large double-storey house across the street. 'It was a terrible thing.'

There was an awkward silence as they both stood looking across the road.

Nick waited another moment then said, 'So … this is your mother's house?'

'Yes, my stepmother's, actually. I'm looking after it while she's away.'

'Where's she gone?'

'I'm sorry, Mr Jarratt. I don't know.'

'The cops have been staking out this place, waiting for her to get back,' Nick said. 'Did you talk to them?'

'No. I saw them sitting in their car for a few days, so I just drove past and didn't go in.'

'Why?'

'I told you before, Mr Jarratt! I don't like them and I don't trust them!'

'They might come back,' Nick said.

'Maybe. Yes. Maybe.' She pondered for a moment and became distant. Then she sparked up.

'So, Mr Jarratt, what would you like to see?' she asked and a sly smile crossed her face as she climbed the wide stairs in front of him leading to the front door.

'Ah …' Nick was lost for words for a moment. 'Could I see Alex's room, please?'

'Sure,' she responded.

She unlocked the huge front doors and they entered

a large foyer. A magnificent marble staircase ran up to the second floor. Expensive paintings hung on polished, wood-panelled walls. Rooms seemed to run off in every direction.

'Wow, beautiful house!' Nick said and puffed out his cheeks.

'Yes, she keeps it in good order.'

She walked ahead, climbed the stairs and opened the door to a bedroom on the left.

'This is it,' she said and stood to one side to usher Nick through. 'Looking for anything special?'

'No, not really. I just thought there might be something here he would especially come back for.'

'Oh,' she muttered.

He took a couple of steps in and stopped.

Posters of rock bands such as Green Day, the Foo Fighters and Radiohead were plastered on every wall. Over the bed hung a large poster of a topless celebrity Nick didn't recognise. In it she was trying unsuccessfully to cover her tiny boobs. Jessica saw him looking at it and reddened slightly.

'He was sixteen when he put that one up. His mother didn't approve, but he insisted.'

'No problem,' Nick said. 'Typical for a growing boy!'

He walked past a Fender Strat and Marshall amp and over to the dressing table. The large mirror had a sticker of Bart Simpson mooning everyone with the caption 'Don't Butt In'. He opened the top drawer. In it were pencils and

Texta pens together with a writing pad. He slid open the bottom drawer. There was a thick woollen jumper on top. He lifted it out and put it on the floor.

'Oh! That's where they are!' Jessica said as she stood behind Nick.

She bent down and picked up a pair of skimpy black knickers from the drawer and then saw a pink pair and grabbed them as well.

'I thought I'd lost them, or that someone had maybe taken them off the clothesline!'

But Nick wasn't listening. He pushed some other clothes aside and found something large and hard. He grabbed it by the handle and took the hammer out of the drawer. He examined the head and the claw but there was nothing there to indicate it had been used to strike anyone. He put it back.

'Do you know why he'd have a hammer in his drawer?'

'No, I'm sorry. I've got no idea.'

Nick checked out the rest of the bedroom.

'Thanks,' he said when he'd finished.

Jessica let Nick pass and then closed the bedroom door. They started downstairs.

'Look, Miss D— Jessica. I know Alex has had a troubled past.'

A worried expression crossed her face. 'Yes, he has.'

'He's escaped from Aimtree mental hospital, hasn't he?'

'Yes,' she admitted and lowered her eyes, 'I should have told you before, but I was just so worried about him!'

They walked down to the ground floor.

'He wasn't staying with you, was he?' Nick asked.

'No,' she said. 'I'm sorry I lied to you!' Tears started to form in her eyes and she took a lace handkerchief from her handbag and pressed it to them.

'I don't know where he is and I'm so worried!' she said.

Nick put his hand on her shoulder and she pressed herself against him.

'Can you help me, please, Mr Jarratt?'

'Sure, I'll do my best.'

'Would you stay a little while and sit with me? It's very hot outside and we could have a drink. I have an extensive bar.'

A surge of adrenaline raced through Nick's body. Memories of making a wrong decision on that fateful night outside the South Melbourne murder house came flooding back. He knew he shouldn't stay. The obvious answer was *No*, but it was just a drink, he told himself. It would probably be all right. Besides, she had the car and he couldn't walk back to the city.

Downstairs in the luxurious lounge room Nick sat on a sumptuous Chesterfield sofa. Ice cubes tinkled as Jessica brought over two tumblers of Grand Marnier.

'Bottom's up,' she said as she sipped at the alcohol and playfully jiggled the ice cubes in the glass.

Nick took a mouthful and smiled back at her.

'Starting to feel better?' he asked.

'I'm a lot better now you're here with me. It's a big house.

I get lonely, you know!'

She put her glass on the coffee table in front of them, smiled at Nick, sat down and put her hand on his knee.

It was now or never he thought. He could get up and leave, or he could stay. Part of his brain was screaming at him saying, *This isn't right! Not with a client. Stay emotionally detached!* The other side of his brain was screaming, *She's hot to trot. Go for it!*

He put his drink on the table and gently put his hand on hers.

'Jessica ... Miss Downton.' He decided to revert back to being formal with her. 'I can stay a little while, but I need to keep this at a professional level, I hope you don't mind.'

He moved her hand away and smiled, hoping the rejection didn't offend her.

'I understand,' she said softly.

She finished her drink then stood up and started to unbutton her shirt.

'It's so hot!' she said and let the shirt fall to the floor in front of him. 'I'm going to have a shower. I'll drive you back to your office afterwards, okay?' She continued to take off her clothes.

Nick nodded meekly. She walked off a few steps, stopped and then turned around. By now she was completely naked.

'But if you change your mind, I'm just down there in the bathroom,' she pointed towards a long corridor. 'It's quite a large shower, plenty of room for two!' Her smile got wider and she raised her eyebrows slightly.

Nick watched her bottom doing figure eights as she walked off. His mind was racing. He drank the last of the alcohol in one swallow, waited until he heard the water running and then reached for his phone.

'Rosalie.'

'Yes Nick!'

'I'll be back later this afternoon, but I'm not sure when. Take any calls and check my diary for any appointments. Let them know I'll be in first thing in the morning, please.'

'Sure thing, Nick,' she said, then added, 'is everything all right?'

'Yeah, yeah, no problems. Something's come up and I want to check it out.'

'Nick,' Rosalie said with a worried tone in her voice, 'you've got more of those weird emails.'

He didn't say anything.

'Whoever it is says he knows where you are, what you're doing, who you're doin' it with, where you work and where you live! It's scary, Nick!'

Nick could hear the concern in her voice.

'Okay Rosalie, I'll check them out first thing tomorrow. Look. Why don't you take the rest of the day off. I'll sort it out tomorrow.'

'Okay, Nick, I'll see you tomorrow. Bye, bye.'

Nick hung up. He could still hear the shower running so he decided to take a look around.

He walked into the kitchen. Machetes, knives and other sharp utensils hung above the kitchen counter from a large rectangular hanging bar. He popped his head into the walk-in pantry and then stepped back into the kitchen and opened the top drawer. It was filled with cutlery. He opened the one below. There were more kitchen implements in it. He was about to close it when he noticed a black rubber handle. He pulled it out. It was another hammer, but this one was covered with a dry and flaky red-brown substance.

A voice came from behind. 'Are you checking out my place?'

Jessica stood behind Nick with her wet hair wrapped in a towel. The rest of her was loosely covered with a white towelling robe that fell open slightly as she spoke.

Nick quickly pushed the hammer back into the drawer.

'Ah, no!' he said in a startled voice. 'I was … I was looking for a glass. I thought I'd get some water.'

She looked at him suspiciously. 'The glasses are in the overhead cupboards.' She pointed and the robe slid open even further, exposing more flesh.

'Oh, okay, thanks!' Nick opened the cupboard, took out a glass and filled it from the kitchen tap.

'I won't be long,' she said and walked away. 'I'll just get dressed and drive you back to your office.'

* * *

On the way to the city she looked over to Nick and asked, 'When I left your office the other day …'

'Yeah?' Nick said, distracted by the incredible houses

they were driving past.

'There was a blonde woman that got into the lift.'

Nick snapped back to attention. 'Yes, so what?'

Her voice took on a harsher tone, 'Who was she?'

'Just a …' Nick was going to say *friend*, but then thought better of it. 'Just another client. She's from an accounting firm.'

He didn't know why he'd lied, but something told him that he didn't want to start revealing parts of his private life to her.

'Oh!' She looked back at the road. 'I thought it might have been a friend – a girlfriend.'

Nick just smiled at her and slowly shook his head. What was she getting at? Why the need to know? Why was she coming on to him?

They didn't speak for the rest of the drive as they made their way into the sweltering heat of the CBD.

22

ANOTHER MURDER

At eight o'clock the next morning, Nick opened up his computer and started to read the emails. Rosalie was standing behind him looking over his shoulder.

'See, there they are! Read them, Nick. They're frightening, some of them!'

'Okay Rosalie, give me a chance!'

Nick scrolled down the screen to where Rosalie pointed and clicked on them:

First email - Jarratt you fuckhead! You think I don't know what you're doing! And who you're doing it with!

Second email - I've seen you with that slut. I know what you're doing with her! I'm gonna hammer her! That witch at reception's gonna get it too!

Third email - Hey Jarratt you piece of shit! I know where you work. I've been there! Yeah, didn't know that did you! Oh yeah, the tart and the kid are also gonna get it! Watch the news Jarratt – someone we know really well is gonna get it today! What you gonna do about it, Jarratt?

Fourth email (sent early this morning) - Still looking, Jarratt? Told ya someone's gonna get it, right in the head! You're gonna find me all right – just look behind ya!

Both Nick and Rosalie turned around and looked at the window overlooking Swanston Street as though they would see someone there.

The fourth email continued – I bet you looked!

'What are you going to do, Nick?' asked Rosalie. 'Those emails scare me!'

They walked to Rosalie's desk.

'Look Rosalie, can you find someone to see if they can track down who sent them? There's gotta be someone in the city who can do that. Also, contact the security company and get them to check out the overnight alarm; see if it's working okay. He says he's been in here, but I don't know how. It could only be at night when we're not here.'

'Okay, Nick. I know someone who can check out the email address. But the alarm – I set it every time I leave, I never forget.'

'That's okay, Rosalie, I'm not blaming you.'

'Nick, he said he would hurt me too!'

'Look, Rosalie. Best thing to do is to make sure you leave when I leave. That way you're not here by yourself.'

Rosalie steeled herself. 'Nick, I don't think that's necessary. I've never told you, but I've got a gun!'

'What?'

'In my top drawer.'

Rosalie slowly opened the drawer and took out the

revolver.

'Jesus, Rosalie!' Nick gasped.

He thought he was the only one with a gun in the office.

'I know, I should have told you! I know how to use it, and … if he comes in here and threatens me, I *will* use it Nick!'

Nick heard the tone of her voice and was about to comment when he got a call on his mobile. It was Claudette.

'Nick!'

'Hi Claud, you don't sound so good. Something the matter?'

There was a pause. 'Yes,' she said and her voice trembled. Nick started to worry.

'Are you okay?'

'No, I'm not! My apartment! Someone's been in here, Nick. The place is a mess!' She sounded like she was on the verge of tears.

'Where are you now?'

'I'm here – in the apartment! I'm scared, Nick. Can you come here now? Please? I don't know what to do. Please, Nick!'

'Sure, sure thing Claud! I'll leave now. I should be there in fifteen – all right?'

'Thanks, Nick. Thank you!' she said and hung up.

Nick strode over to the lift. 'Rosalie I gotta go! It's Claudette. Sounds like her apartment's been gone over!'

Rosalie looked at him and frowned. 'You don't suppose it could be him, do you Nick?'

'I don't know, Rosalie!'

He stopped at the door. 'Rosalie, I'll call you on my way back. Don't shoot anyone while I'm gone, okay?'

'I won't, Nick. Not unless someone attacks me! Then I'll shoot 'em all right, you can bet on it!'

Rosalie watched him leave and the worried expression never left her face.

* * *

Claudette's apartment was a disaster. There were clothes strewn all over the bedroom floor, the chairs in the kitchen had been overturned and the kitchen table was on its side. But the most worrying thing for Nick was the mirror in Claudette's bathroom.

He stood there unable to move as he looked at the red lipstick scrawled all over it. There were drawings of a hammer and a pair of bare breasts, but most worrying of all were the words

No sense running. It's way too late for running.

Claudette grabbed Nick's arm.

'It's weird and disgusting isn't it?' she said and looked up at him.

He didn't answer. He was fixated on the mirror.

'Nick! Nick! Are you okay?' she said, shaking his arm.

'Yeah, yeah! Sorry, Claud,' he said as he snapped out of it.

'When did this happen?'

'Must have been last night, I was staying with my mother. She's not well.'

'Did anything get taken?'

'I'm not sure. I don't think so.'

'How'd they get in?'

'I don't know!' Claudette said. 'Nothing's been forced or smashed. I guess through the window over the toilet. I leave it open most of the time, you know, for fresh air.' She looked like she was going to cry.

'Okay, Claud. Okay.' Nick was going to say something sharp, then thought better of it. 'Maybe, just keep it closed from now on.'

She didn't answer but kept a tight hold of his arm.

'You got an alarm?' he asked.

'No,' she replied. 'The agent told me this was a really safe neighbourhood and I wouldn't need one.'

Nick slowly shook his head. 'Okay,' he muttered under his breath.

'Look, I think it's best if you stay with me for a night or two. I'll organise an alarm system and put better locks on the doors, maybe some bars on the back windows as well.'

'Thanks, Nick,' she said and squeezed his arm. 'I'll get some stuff together. If I can find anything!'

They spent some time searching through the mess, trying to gather what she needed by way of clothes and toiletries. He told Claudette to not disturb too much of the scene if she could help it, as he'd contact Drury and get him to send a forensics team over to have a look.

They were driving back to Nick's apartment when his phone rang. Nick pressed the 'accept call' button on the steering wheel and the radio immediately shut down; Pete Drury's voice blared out through the car speakers.

'Nick!'

'G'day, Pete, I was gonna call you! What's up?'

'Mate, you better get over to Fairview Park in Hawthorn. There's been a murder. Looks like your boy's been at it again! The old girl who lived next door. The one he bashed a few years ago. Well, she's dead! Head's been caved in with a blunt instrument, probably a hammer.'

'Whoa,' Nick whispered under his breath. 'Okay Pete, I'll be there asap.'

Drury hung up and the car's radio automatically kicked back in.

'Was that Pete Drury?' Claudette asked.

'Yes,' Nick replied. 'Looks like we're gonna take a detour.'

* * *

The scene in the park was chaotic. Cop cars were every-where, lights flashing. They had the murder scene taped off. Drury saw Nick approaching and lifted the tape for him.

They walked over to where the old woman was on her side lying under some low bushes. Blood was spattered all over the place, the main source being the gaping wounds in her head. It looked as if her skull had been broken open.

Blood and bits of brain had run out and seeped into the lush green grass. A policewoman held a dog by its leash. It was straining to get back to the old woman.

'So, it's definitely the old girl?' Nick asked.

'Yep,' Drury replied. 'Thelma Ashby, same one he bashed years ago. Looks like she walked the dog every afternoon. Guess he found out her routine, followed her and …' Drury just pointed and didn't finish the sentence.

Nick checked out the scene, careful not to get in the way of the forensics team who were painstakingly picking through the grass. He took one last look then walked away with Drury.

'Could have been anyone, really!' Nick said. 'I mean if she walks alone in the park, any nutter could have done this.'

Drury shook his head.

'Too much of a coincidence for us. Downton escapes from Aimtree and Thelma Ashby gets killed with what looks like a hammer? It's him all right! We just gotta find him. We're gonna do a media release later on today and get a picture of him on every news channel and in every newspaper. We need help finding him. He's bloody crafty!'

They walked over to Claudette, who was standing on the other side of the police tape.

'Was it an old lady?' she asked.

'What's she doin' here?' Drury snapped.

'Sorry, Pete!' Nick said.

'Yeah, Claud. It is.' Nick said, ducking under the tape

and taking Claudette's hand as they headed back to the car.

A voice came from the cluster of police and detectives standing nearby.

'Hey Jarratt!' It was Grant Davidson, Nick's old nemesis from the police force. 'I see ya still got that little piece of fluff!' he yelled.

Nick and Claudette walked on but Davidson called out again, this time directed towards Claudette.

'Lookin' good, sweetheart! But not as good as when you're in the back of a divvy van!' He laughed and looked to his colleagues, who joined in. 'Keepin' it well dusted are ya?' he snorted again.

A couple of cops who knew Nick and Claudette from their days at the station watched them walk past and silently laughed to one another. Nick stopped and was about to turn around and confront Davidson but Claudette grabbed his arm.

'Don't worry about him, Nick! He's a loser. He always was.'

Nick gritted his teeth but took her advice and kept walking. Once they were inside his car he turned to Claudette.

'I hate that prick!' he said as he started the engine.

'Don't worry about him!' Claudette said and patted his arm.

When it looked like he'd settled down she asked, 'But how come Drury rang *you* about the old lady?'

Nick didn't answer.

Back at his apartment in Flinders Street, Nick used his key to open the door to the private lift. He ushered Claudette in and hit the button for the first floor. It creaked and clanged as it made its way up and soon the doors opened up directly into the huge lounge area.

Claudette walked in and put her overnight bag on one of the chairs then looked over at Flinders Street railway station across the road. She turned to Nick and said, 'Thanks for letting me stay.'

He smiled at her. 'No worries, Claud, I'm really pleased to have you with me.'

A concerned look crossed her face. 'Nick, you never did say why Pete Drury called you to have a look at that murder scene.'

Nick walked over to the kitchenette and opened an overhead cupboard. He took out two wine glasses and placed them on the table, which served as the breakfast, lunch and dinner table.

'Sav blanc?'

'Yes please,' she replied.

He poured the wine and brought the glasses over to where she was sitting.

'Remember I said I had a client whose stepbrother was missing – you know, the one who gave you the evil eye?'

'Yes,' Claudette answered, casually sipping the cold wine.

'Well, it turns out her stepbrother has done a couple of stints in Aimtree House, the mental hospital. The first time for bashing the same old lady we saw in the park today. He didn't kill her then, but he's escaped and it looks like he might have finished what he started a few years ago.'

'Oh really,' Claudette said softly and looked worried. 'Do you think he'll come after you?'

Nick hesitated and put his hand on hers, not really sure how to answer her.

'No … I don't think so,' he said and tried to sound re-assuring, but his mind was racing. Then he added, 'Claud, you can stay here as long as you like. I mean, we should have done this ages ago. You don't ever have to leave if you don't want to!'

She went red in the face. 'Thanks Nick,' she said and smiled back at him.

'Your car's still at your place, I can get it for you.'

'Don't worry, I'm waitressing at the Sparkling Café. It's just a quick tram ride down Collins Street. I'll get it later.'

'Okay,' Nick said and sipped his wine. 'Oh! I forgot to tell you; I've updated the apartment.'

'How?' she asked looking around.

'I bought a new bed,' Nick smiled and added, 'it's queen size and really comfy.'

A smile crossed her lips. She slowly shook her head and finished her glass.

'Okay, I guess we'll have to test it out sometime,' she said and rolled her eyes.

Then she held her glass up and asked, 'What does a girl have to do to get a refill around here?'

23

INTERVIEW WITH DR SHELTON

Nick pulled up out the front of Jeffrey Shelton's practice in Portman Street, Oakleigh. It looked like it had been a charming little place in its heyday, but that had clearly been a long time ago. He got out of his car and walked along the cracked footpath leading to the dilapidated front door. A weathered brass plaque was nailed to the entrance claiming Shelton's right to the title Doctor of Psychiatry.

A bell tinkled above the door as he opened it and stepped inside. There was no receptionist. He walked into the entrance hall, which had once been the lounge room, and waited. He could hear Shelton on the phone in another room down the hall.

'Just a minute!' Shelton called out, then resumed his phone call.

Nick decided to have a quick look around. The walls were cracked in places and the paint job looked grubby and chipped. Shelton's degree from Melbourne University hung on the wall together with other certificates and a plaque from a local charity thanking him for a generous donation. A vase with faded plastic flowers covered in dust stood on a low table next to magazines that were years old. Outside through the grime-covered windows he could see Shelton's shiny black Mercedes convertible parked in the weedy driveway. It clearly showed where Shelton's priorities were.

He heard Shelton finish his phone call and hang up. His shoes sounded loud on the bare floorboards as he walked into the reception area.

'Ah! Detective Jarratt, how nice to see you!' Shelton said and held out his hand.

He was dressed in a slim-fitting black suit. The tie, a flaming red, was a noticeable contrast to his elegantly styled greying hair, moustache and goatee beard.

Nick shook Shelton's hand. 'Private detective – private investigator actually. I'm not the police!'

'Oh okay,' Shelton smiled. 'Please, come down to my room.'

Nick followed Shelton along the narrow passageway and into a small office. Shelton sat at the far side of a large desk. Behind him on bare wooden shelves, mountains of files were arranged haphazardly. On the wall hung a photo of Shelton receiving his Bachelor's degree. It showed him smiling for the camera with his mortar board slanting ever so slightly to one side.

He motioned to Nick to sit in the visitor's chair.

'So how can I help you de— Mr Jarratt?'

'Like I said on the phone, doctor, I'm looking for Alex Downton. I believe he was a patient of yours at Aimtree House?'

'Yes, yes that's right. I've been with him for a number of years. He's been there on two separate occasions, you know.'

Nick nodded.

Shelton continued, 'Bad thing that he's escaped. He could be confused and worried right now. He may not know where he is.'

'More like we – the public, that is – are worried about where he is!' said Nick. 'He's been convicted of grievous bodily harm and a double murder, as you know.'

Shelton looked into the distance and rubbed his goatee beard. 'Yes,' he said thoughtfully. 'He's a troubled boy, Mr Jarratt. He needs constant treatment.' Shelton looked at Nick. 'So, how do you think I can help?'

'There was another murder yesterday.'

'Oh?' Shelton said, surprised.

'Thelma Ashby,' Nick explained.

Shelton looked at Nick, waiting for him to elaborate.

'The old lady he assaulted a few years ago. She was bludgeoned to death in a park near her home yesterday afternoon.'

Shelton stared at Nick and took a moment to speak. 'And you think it was Alex?' he asked, obviously not convinced by Nick's implication.

'Got all the hallmarks of Downton,' Nick said. 'And it's

the same old lady!'

'Maybe Tyson …' Shelton muttered to himself.

Nick wondered what Shelton was on about. He asked, 'Well, do you have any idea where he might be or where he might go?'

Shelton leant back in his chair.

'Truth is, Mr Jarratt, he could be anywhere, but I doubt he's travelled too far. I believe he might try to find his way back to his home. He was staying there with his mother and stepfather before he was involved in those terrible incidents,' Shelton said and shifted in his chair.

'Well, there's no sign of him at the house – he seems to have just vanished!' Nick said.

'Hmm,' Shelton murmured and said half to himself, 'he, Tyson that is, can be very resourceful.' He hesitated for a moment and said, 'You know, his mother, Helen, used to come to see Alex at Aimtree, but the stepfather never did.'

This time it was Nick's turn to sit back and pause.

'What about Jessica, did she ever visit?

'Not that I'm aware of. Apparently she was there at the start, when he was first admitted, but his mother was always very protective of him. She was the only one I ever saw visit him.'

Nick nodded. 'Well, there's a problem with that as well, doctor.'

'What's that?' Shelton said and sat forward.

'There's no sign of his mother or the stepfather. They both seem to have just disappeared.'

Shelton leant back in his chair and stared up at the ceiling seemingly lost in his own thoughts once more.

Nick snapped him out of it. 'I've been contacted by his stepsister, Jessica. She says he's supposed to be staying with her.'

Nick said this knowing that Jessica had since confessed that it was a lie, but he wanted to see how Shelton would react.

'Jessica?' Shelton said as he jerked back to reality. 'Like I said, I'm sure she never visited him, but he did mention her a few times. She's quite a bit older than Alex you know; actually, she's not that much younger than his mother.' Shelton paused, 'Funny thing,' he said as he looked searchingly at Nick. 'I never heard that he was supposed to be staying with Jessica. When was that?'

'I don't know,' said Nick. 'She just said he was supposed to be with her, but I don't see how that could be possible if he was in Aimtree.'

'You don't suppose she knew he was going to escape, do you Mr Jarratt?' Shelton seemed more interested now.

Nick shrugged. A knot was starting to form in his belly. This case was getting stranger by the minute. He changed the subject.

'I understand he overpowered a nurse at the hospital. Desiree Thompson, was it?'

'Yes, he did, but he didn't kill her. That was also Tyson no doubt,' Shelton replied.

'Tyson?' Nick repeated and frowned. 'Who's Tyson?'

'Oh, you don't know?' Shelton reached forward and opened a file on his desk marked 'Alex Downton'.

'Don't know what, doc?'

'Alex has a particular condition known as DID.'

Nick frowned as he took this information in. 'DID – what's that?'

'Dissociative identity disorder.'

Nick sat silently waiting for him to explain.

'It used to be called multiple personality disorder,' Shelton said, then paused. 'You see, Mr Jarratt, Alex has more than one active personality.'

Nick's frown got deeper. 'How do you mean?'

'There is Alex the stutterer who likes to sit in his room, read his books and does not socialise very much. Then there's a second personality, Tyson, who is a brutal bully, and, I believe, a murderer. Alex used to refer to yet another persona as the Naughty Boy. I believe it was that one who hit Thelma Ashby with the spade back when he was thirteen. But you see that personality has been pushed into the background by a new and even more vicious one – Tyson.' Shelton tapped his head as he spoke to Nick. 'This is all happening in Alex's mind, you understand, Mr Jarratt. He's a very sick boy.'

Shelton looked at Nick with a superior smile.

Nick sat forward. 'So, what can you tell me about Tyson?'

'When Tyson comes forward Alex also gets pushed into the background. This is called "switching", to use the medical parlance.' Shelton paused to make sure Nick was taking it all in.

He went on. 'Tyson is much stronger than Alex and seems to come forward when there is trouble, or perceived trouble. He can be very violent. He is unpredictable; however, he is a very good planner. Also – interestingly – Tyson, like the Naughty Boy, doesn't stutter. I believe it was Tyson who escaped from Aimtree. He has the organisational capability and strength to accomplish such a task.'

Nick rubbed his forehead. 'So, do we know where Tyson might go?'

Shelton shook his head. 'Same problem. He could go anywhere. As I said, he is very resourceful. Our only chance would be if he fades into the background and Alex comes forward. Alex would be caught very easily.'

Nick was becoming more concerned.

'So, you believe it's Tyson who is capable of murder?'

'Oh yes, very much so!' Shelton said enthusiastically. 'He just needs a target, someone that he perceives has done him wrong, or upset him, or simply someone that he just doesn't like the look of. That's all it takes.'

'But he didn't kill the nurse on the night he escaped.'

'No, but I'm not totally surprised by that. He's …' Shelton paused again. 'Alex is very fond of Desiree Thompson. He likes her very much. Perhaps he convinced Tyson not to kill her.' Then Shelton added, 'It's her small breasts, you know.'

'What?' Nick asked perplexed.

'Yes, he likes the ones with small breasts.' Shelton pursed

his lips as he mentioned this fact. 'It reminds him of a girl he considered to be his girlfriend. He killed her, you know, although he has always denied doing it.'

Nick shook his head, considering this last remark, then said, 'A few years ago a nurse that worked at Aimtree, Audrey Withers, was bashed to death in her house in South Melbourne. Records at Aimtree show she looked after Downton when he was there.'

Shelton nodded.

'Did she have little boobs as well?'

Shelton sat back in his chair thinking. 'Well ... yes, as a matter of fact she did,' Shelton said and stared at Nick. 'Come to think of it, Nurse Thompson is not unlike Audrey Withers. In a way they are quite similar.'

Nick was getting frustrated. 'Look, doc, is there anything you can tell me that could help?'

Shelton stared at Nick and considered his request for a moment.

'I'm not supposed to divulge patient details or comment about their family, but I guess this is a special circumstance. You won't tell anyone if I let you in on some confidential information, will you?'

'I'll keep whatever you tell me to myself, but I can't guarantee I won't use it to find Downton.'

'Okay then,' Shelton said. Returning to the file on his desk, he thumbed through a number of pages and pulled out three that were paper clipped together marked 'History and Family Tree'. He put it on the desk, read it briefly then looked back up at Nick.

'When I first started treating Alex, I did some digging in his ancestry. His condition is rare, but I believe it's hereditary. There is a line of mental illness that runs through the family, but it only turns up every so often. It appears to be stronger on the female side but has occasionally spilt over to the males. I have found records of a maternal great-grandmother being institutionalised and then sketchy records of the mother before her. It looks as though she was also diagnosed as being mad. The only male relative I can find with similar problems was a great uncle who was put in a lunatic asylum when he was sixteen years old. He never came out, you know. He died there.'

Nick took this in. 'So, there's a track record of insanity in the family and Alex was the unlucky one?'

'Yes, it looks that way.'

'Can he be cured?'

'I have been trying an experi—, ah, a new treatment on him, which I believe was having very positive results, but there is a long way to go. I need to get him back there.'

'I know, doc. We all need to get him back there!'

24

CHANCE SIGHTING

At 6:30pm the next night in Young & Jackson, Nick headed up to Chloe's Brasserie for dinner. He'd been waiting in the bar downstairs when he got a call from Pete Drury to say he'd be late and would catch up with him around 9:00pm.

Nick walked over to the small bar to grab a quick beer before being shown to his table. In the crowd of half a dozen people also waiting, he saw a young man standing at the corner of the bar by himself. He was staring at the full-length picture of the naked Chloe. He seemed fixated on her. Nick moved closer to get a better look at him when Alex Downton spotted him and bolted.

'Wait!' yelled Nick.

But Downton was quick. He pushed past the waitresses and raced downstairs with Nick hot on his heels. Out on Swanston Street, Nick lost him in the crowd momentarily, then saw him again running between the traffic across Flinders Street. Nick followed but got slowed down at the lights as a tram rumbled past. He ran around the back of it and saw Downton leap up the stairs of the railway station. Nick ran against the traffic. Horns blared and tyres screeched as he darted between the cars. He saw Downton jump the ticket gate and head into the station proper. Nick followed. A guard stood in his way.

'Ticket!'

'Look, mate – I've gotta catch that guy!'

Nick pointed and when the guard turned to see who he was pointing at, Nick jumped the gate.

'Hey!' the guard yelled, but Nick kept running.

He guessed at which ramp Downton had taken and took the one heading to platforms 4 & 5. He flew down the escalator steps two at a time, pushed his way through the crowd and made it onto the platform. He started searching amongst the sea of people waiting for the Lilydale train. He strode from one end to the other but there was no sign of him. He looked over the tracks and saw Downton standing one platform away on numbers 6 & 7. Alex spotted Nick and stood still for a moment.

Nick's heart was thumping in his chest. He cupped his hands and yelled, 'Alex – it's okay, I won't hurt you!'

Alex stared back at Nick, but didn't speak.

Nick ducked out of the way as a cart full of luggage rumbled past. He moved closer to the edge of the platform in an attempt to make himself heard over the flood of announcements bellowing out all through the station.

'Alex. I can help you!'

Alex looked over at him, slowly shook his head and yelled back, 'I-I w-w-want Jessie! I w-want my m-m-mother!'

'I can help you find them!' Nick shouted. 'Let me help you!'

Alex just stood there and started to shake his head. The hiss and screech of a train braking as it entered the station split the air. Then Nick saw Downton's face change to a scowl and a low guttural voice escaped his lips.

'You won't help me! You'll just send me back there. I'm never going back!' Tyson yelled and clenched his fists. 'They blame me for everything. Everything!'

Nick was going to shout back when an announcement blared out from the overhead speakers.

Stand clear, please. The train arriving on platform 6 is the Pakenham line train, Pakenham train arriving on platform 6, stand clear.

The suburban train rushed in. Nick could see Downton intermittently through the carriage windows as the train slowed to a stop. But when he looked again, he was gone.

Nick couldn't tell if Alex had run down the ramp or entered one of the train carriages. Nick raced around to platform 6 & 7, but found no sign of him. He briefly checked each carriage on the Pakenham line train as best he could, but he was not there. Within seconds the train left the station. Nick checked the rails that ran alongside the platform but there was no one hiding there either. It was as though Downton had simply vanished.

Nick made his way up the escalators and towards the exit. He waited a couple of minutes until he saw a gate that wasn't being monitored, climbed over it, crossed Flinders Street and walked into the crowded front bar of Young & Jackson. Pete Drury spotted him as he walked through the door.

'Nick!' he called out and waved.

'I thought you were gonna be late!' Nick said as he walked over to Drury. 'Nine o'clock or thereabouts.'

Drury smiled back at him. 'Yeah, well I'm very efficient you know. I get things done quicker than most.'

Nick said, 'I've just seen our man!'

'Who?'

'Downton – just now! I lost him in the station.' Nick pointed back over his shoulder towards Flinders Street Station.

Drury took his mobile phone out of his pocket. 'I'll call the boys!'

'Hang on, you said you'd give me a chance to get him!'

'Sorry, mate, too many murders. Too much grief. We've already got a team looking for him. Jesus, Nick, we've gotta catch this bloke!' Drury began to punch numbers on his phone, then said, 'Did he catch a train?'

'Yeah, probably,' Nick said, 'Pakenham line – but who knows where he'd get off.'

Drury made the call then hung up.

'So, you're not on the team?' Nick asked.

'Well, I am, but I put a young *brainiac* in charge. He's

been at me to run a significant case for a while, and this looked like something he could get his teeth into.'

Drury nodded to himself then added, 'I'll keep pace with him, though, but monitor it from the sidelines and not get in his way. Besides, I'm too bloody old these days to be runnin' round!'

* * *

Upstairs in Chloe's Brasserie, Nick and Drury were again enjoying the restaurant's best steak.

Nick said, 'I saw Shelton yesterday.'

Drury looked up from his dinner with a quizzical look on his face, kept chewing and didn't speak.

'Shelton – Dr Shelton. Downton's shrink,' Nick prompted.

'Oh, yeah,' Drury said as he pushed more eye fillet into his mouth. 'What did he have to say for himself?'

'Looks like Downton's got a personality disorder.'

'Wouldn't think that's all he's got!' Drury said and washed down his mouthful with the remainder of his beer.

'Shelton told me he's got DID.'

Drury looked at Nick, raised one eyebrow and cut off another piece of meat.

'Dissociative identity disorder – multiple personalities,' Nick added. 'Apparently he's got a good one and a bad one. The bad one does the killing.'

'Strewth!' Drury exclaimed, then added, 'Didn't say where he might be, did he?'

Nick shook his head and cut off a generous portion of the prime meat. 'Downton yelled out to me at the station.'

'Oh! What'd he say?'

'First of all, he said he wanted Jessie and then his mother, then he said he wasn't gonna let me help him. He reckoned I was gonna put him back in Aimtree!'

'Damn right!' remarked Drury.

'Mmm,' Nick mused. 'Guess he's not that dumb after all!'

There was silence as the men continued eating. The waiter brought over the wine list. Nick ordered the house shiraz for both of them.

'Did you find out anything?' Nick asked.

'Well, yeah, as a matter of fact I have,' Drury said and wiped his mouth with a serviette. 'We can't find Helen Downton, Alex's mother, but we did find his stepfather.'

'So?'

Drury went back to eating. 'Found him in his car,' Drury chewed then swallowed. 'Deceased.'

'Car crash?' Nick asked.

'Nope. Found him in the underground car park where he works. Been there for days. Head had been bashed in. Looks like someone – your boy, probably – caught up with him while he was sitting behind the wheel. The driver's side window was smashed in and there was poor old Victor, sitting there dead with his brains in his lap.'

He looked over at Nick, shrugged his shoulders and washed down another piece of partially cooked steak with a mouthful of red wine, which had arrived at the table.

25

BREAK-IN

A couple of days later Nick took a call on his mobile. There was no Caller ID.

'Hello? Who's this?'

'Nick!'

It was Angie. Nick was surprised. She sounded upset.

'What's up?' he asked.

'Someone broke in last night!'

'What! Are you okay? Is *Liam* okay?'

'Yes, yes. But I'm worried, Nick!'

There was a vulnerability in her voice Nick hadn't heard for years. It touched a part of him he'd kept hidden since their breakup. Deep down he still wanted to help her, wanted to protect her, but too much raging water had passed under the bridge for that.

'Did they take anything?' he asked in a soft voice hoping it might help her to calm down.

'No, not that I'm aware of, but they left a note.'

'What ... what sort of note?' Nick's heart thudded.

'Scrawled on the mirror in my bedroom. They used my lipstick!' Her voice started to tremble.

'What did it say?' He wasn't sure he really wanted to know; too many strange things were already happening.

'It's weird. Says something about being too late to run …'

Nick froze. The dream came rushing back. He was lost for words for a moment.

'Did you call the police?'

'Yes. They were here in the afternoon. That detective mate of yours was here. What's his name … Drury?'

'Yeah, Pete Drury.'

'He said I should call you and let you know.'

Nick was silent for a moment. His mind was racing.

'Where are you now?'

'Still here.'

'What! Didn't they …?'

'It's okay, a policewoman stayed with us.'

'Is she still there?'

'No, she left about an hour ago.'

Nick could hear her breathing heavily.

'Detective Drury said we shouldn't stay here overnight – not until I get a security door and steel window shutters.'

'Where are you going to stay?' Nick paused. 'At your mother's?'

'No, she's overseas and she's got a house sitter staying. I don't suppose … I don't suppose we could stay with you, could we?'

Angie's voice was pleading. His stomach lurched. He had to tell her Claudette was staying with him, but his mind wandered momentarily. In a different time, a different universe, if things hadn't worked out as they had, if she'd coped better with the newborn, if he hadn't done what he'd done – he could say it was fine for her and Liam to stay. Perhaps it would have been the start of a reconciliation between them. But it was too late for any of that. The universe had moved on, and he just had to deal with it.

'I'm sorry Angie, but I've got Clau—'

'Oh, don't worry about it!' she spat the words out. 'I should've known you'd have *her* there!'

'Look, I'm sorry. I can organise a room in a hotel just around the corner from me.'

He could feel her getting angrier on the other end of the line; no doubt she was about to give him another blast. Then he remembered what Liam had said about a new boyfriend and cut her off.

'What about Kelvin? Can't he help?'

Her voice broke as she spoke. 'Kelvin left me after the break-in. He said he didn't want to get involved in any crap that you might have had a hand in!'

'What? He just left you?'

'Yes,' she said trying not to cry into the phone.

'Some bloody hero!' he said triumphantly.

He knew what he said hurt her and wished he could have taken it back. She didn't answer.

'So, how's Liam?'

'Yeah, he's fine, not that you care!'

'Look Angie I do care! I just hardly ever get to see him!'

'You should have thought about that a long time ago! Before you …'

Nick could see this was going nowhere. The old arguments were starting up again and this time he was going to cut it short.

'Look, Angie,' he said sternly. 'I haven't got time for any more bloody quarrels! If you want somewhere to stay I can organise it. Just let me know.'

'Thanks for nothing, Nick! I'll organise myself *and* our son!'

This last comment wasn't lost on Nick.

'Just make sure—' The line went dead. '—that you look after Liam,' Nick continued to say, but he was talking into dead air.

He sighed heavily then rang Pete Drury.

'Drury.'

'Pete, it's me. I just got off the phone to Angie.'

'Yeah, okay Nick, we've been there and had a look.'

'What do you think?'

'I don't like it. She can't stay there. We put a female cop with her last night, but she's gotta get out of there! You got any ideas where she can stay?'

Nick's heart slumped.

'I told her I can organise a hotel room for her and Liam, but she just blew me off! I don't know where she'll stay.'

'Oh,' Drury grunted, 'I'll see what we can organise from here.'

'What do you think, Pete, any idea who did it?'

'Got the trademarks of your boy all over it – lipstick on the mirror and all. But once again we've got no DNA. He's bloody shrewd when it comes to these break-ins!'

26

LUNCHTIME WARNING

The following day Rosalie quickly put away her mobile phone when she heard the lift door close downstairs. Twenty seconds later it opened on the sixth floor and Jessica Downton walked into the reception area.

'Hello Miss Downton,' she said.

'Hello,' Jessica Downton snapped, 'is Mr Jarratt in?'

'No, sorry, he's out to lunch.'

'Oh! His usual haunt – Young & Jackson?'

'Ah,' Rosalie was stunned for a moment, not sure how she knew where Nick ate his meals. 'Yes, that's right.'

Rosalie pointed in the general direction of the hotel.

'Yes, yes, I know it!' Jessica said, then turned on her heel and strode to the lift.

Rosalie shook her head as she watched her leave. She was becoming very wary of Jessica Downton.

* * *

At Young & Jackson, Jessica Downton checked the main bar, and when she saw Nick wasn't having a counter meal there she made her way upstairs to the brasserie. She looked briefly at the full-length picture of Chloe and scoffed, then walked to the entrance of the dining area and scanned the tables. She saw Nick sitting with a friend and walked in.

'Can I help you?' a waiter said, blocking her path.

She didn't answer.

'Do you have a booking, ma'am?' the waiter asked as he continued to stand in her way.

'No!' she said and pushed past him.

She strode over to Nick's table and stood there waiting until he looked up.

'Oh! Miss Downton!' he said.

He put his knife and fork down, grabbed a serviette and wiped his mouth.

She looked down at him. 'Have you made any progress, Mr Jarratt?'

Nick looked at her and then across to Drury.

'I've seen him, but ...'

'What! You've seen him? Where?'

'Well, here, actually, then over at the railway station, but he ran off and I lost him.'

She clutched her handbag. 'So, did you talk to him?'

'Not really. But he did yell out to me that he wanted to see you and his mother, and then he said he didn't want to go back. I presume he meant he didn't want to go back to Aimtree House.'

Nick looked across again at Drury who ignored him and kept eating.

'Mr Jarratt, I'm worried about him.' She paused and looked around the restaurant. 'Please ... Please be careful. He might ... He might do something unexpected and hurt himself, or hurt you!' She clutched her handbag even tighter.

'Thanks,' said Nick, knowing damn well how dangerous Alex could be.

She noticed Pete Drury eyeing off her long legs.

'Jessica Downton,' she said forcefully and extended her hand to Drury.

Drury squeezed her hand. '*Detective* Pete Drury,' he said. 'We're all looking for him, Miss Downton.'

She looked down at him and then ran her eyes over the enormous plate of food. Obviously he wasn't looking for Alex at the moment.

Drury noticed her gaze. 'We've all got to eat, Miss Downton!'

She ignored him.

'I'm worried about my brother, detective!'

'Stepbrother!' Drury corrected her.

She ignored him again. 'He's lost and may be scared. It might make him do something ... something out of the ordinary.'

'Thanks for your advice,' Drury said flatly and went back to his meal. 'Any idea where we can find him?' he asked without looking up and stuffed another piece of steak in his mouth.

'No! I've already told Mr Jarratt that. If I knew where he was I'd get him myself!'

Drury just nodded his head and kept chewing.

She looked down at both men, then turned her back on them and walked out. They watched her leave. Drury waited until she disappeared down the stairs.

'Nice relationship you've got goin' there, Nick! You see many clients at lunchtime?'

Nick shook his head. 'I guess she's just worried where he might be and what he might do.'

'Good set of pins!' Drury remarked, disregarding Nick's comment.

'Yes, she is ah … attractive,' Nick said as he picked up his knife and fork and went back to his lunch.

There was a pregnant pause, then Nick asked, 'Any leads on who broke into Angie's apartment?'

Drury shook his head. 'No. But I still reckon it was your bloke,' he said and finished his mouthful. 'Forensics are still sifting through the mess, and there's another team still looking at Claudette's place as well. Got nothin' in either of them, but they've said they'll keep goin' for another couple of days.'

'Did you guys find a place for Angie and Liam. I—'

'Yeah,' said Drury cutting him off. 'Safe house for a couple of days.'

'Thanks,' Nick said.

Drury grunted then said, 'I see you've organised a *safe*

house for Claudette!'

Nick nodded but didn't answer.

Drury chuckled then took another mouthful. 'You know you've got yourself in deep shit with this one, don't ya!'

'Yeah,' Nick said and looked up from his plate and into the distance.

Drury was right, he thought. Once again he'd got himself in over his head and he wondered just how it all might end.

27

CLOSE ENCOUNTER

A boiling red sun rose in the east and scorched the landscape. The early morning rays caught the clouds building in the west and flushed their dark rumbling underbellies with crimson and orange.

It was 5:30am when Nick got out of bed, careful not to wake Claudette. He showered, shaved and got dressed, but by the time he was ready to leave she had started to stir.

'You're starting early,' she said as she propped herself up against the bedhead and stretched.

'Oh, I'm sorry. I was trying not to wake you.'

She yawned and sat up. 'That's okay.'

Nick looked over at her. What a beauty, he thought.

It had hurt him to tell Angie that she and Liam couldn't stay with him, but when he saw Claudette he wasn't sad about how things had turned out. But he did make a mental note to spend more time with Liam. He'd stuffed a lot of things up in the past and he was determined not to add Liam to that list.

'I want to get to the office early. There are some emails I want to look at. Also, I asked Rosalie to check the alarm system. I want to make sure it's working.' Nick did up the zipper on his trousers. 'Don't worry if you hear a siren, it'll probably be me. Might give some early starters a bit of a jolt!' he laughed.

He walked over and hit the button for the lift. Downstairs the ancient contraption came to life and began its journey upwards.

'You working today?' he asked.

'No. It's my day off, I'm going to stay here and take it easy.'

'Oh, okay, then I'll see you tonight. Let's go out for a meal.'

The lift door opened and Nick got in.

'Sounds good. Bye baby!' she called out.

* * *

In the early morning Nick walked to his office along Swanston Street. The heat was already building, aided by the hot northerly that blustered and howled along the mostly deserted thoroughfare. He got to the ground floor of his office, pressed the button and waited for the lift doors to open. He rode it to the sixth floor and checked the alarm pin pad at the door. A tiny red light was flashing off and on indicating that the alarm was set.

Well, here goes! he thought.

He put the key in the lock and pushed open the door to the reception area. The alarm immediately began to sound a series of warning beeps then ten seconds later, the full siren blasted out, almost deafening him. He quickly walked over to the pin pad, punched in the code and the siren stopped.

Well, there's nothing wrong with that! he thought.

He wondered if it had been okay all along or if Rosalie had got it fixed. He'd ask her when she got in.

He walked over to his desk and saw an icon flashing in the bottom right-hand corner of the computer screen. He clicked on it. The screen sprang into life and highlighted fifteen unread messages. He logged into his email account and began reading them:

'You bastard! No one's gonna catch me!'

'I seen you with that bitch!'

He read the remaining messages. The last one froze him to the bone.

* * *

Claudette got out of the shower, dried off and dressed in light casual clothes. She put on minimal makeup and decided to leave her hair wet. She figured it wouldn't take long to dry in this weather.

She walked out into the large open lounge area and over to the kitchenette to make breakfast when she heard a clanging and banging coming from the ground floor. The lift had cranked into life and was running up to the apartment.

That's funny, she thought, wondering why Nick was coming back so soon.

She took the toaster out of the cupboard and just then her mobile phone rang in the bedroom. She was on her way to answer it when the lift doors opened. A tall figure stood in the dim light. Claudette stopped in her tracks.

'Ah … hi,' she said. 'This is a private apartment. I think you've got the wrong place.' Her voice wavered a little as she spoke.

The tall figure entered the room. 'I haven't got the wrong place! I know exactly where I am, you stupid bitch!'

Claudette didn't move. The phone continued to ring.

The figure was wearing a ski mask and strode towards her swinging what she thought looked like a metal pole or a hammer.

'Wh-wh-what do you want?' she stammered, backing away.

The tall figure walked further into the apartment.

'Please don't hurt me! I've got money, and—'

'I don't want your money, you stupid cow!'

The hammer slammed into a chair knocking it to the floor. The phone rang and rang.

'I want you!'

Claudette realised she had to move and she had to do it now. The bedroom was too far away so it had to be the bathroom. At least there was a latch on the door. The intruder stepped towards her as she raced for the bathroom.

'No sense running!' came the eerie voice. 'It's way too late for running!'

Claudette pushed the door open and then slammed it shut behind her. She screamed as a hammer blow smashed against the wooden panel. Then the door handle started to turn.

'Shit!' she said as she fumbled with the latch. Her hands didn't seem to want to work.

The door handle kept turning and the door opened a crack.

'Come out, bitch!' came the voice.

Claudette pushed hard against the door but couldn't get it to close properly.

'Open the door!' the figure yelled.

She sobbed with terror, then slammed her shoulder against the door. It shut for just an instant and gave her time to twist the privacy switch. She wiped her eyes with the back of her hand. Her heart was in her throat. She backed away from the door and could hear grunting and heaving coming from the other side. She was locked in with no escape. Then she remembered the old fire escape. She climbed up on the toilet cistern and shoved open the frosted glass window. There was hardly enough room for her to get through, but it was the only chance she had.

The door handle rattled as it was twisted and yanked.

'Come out, bitch! Open this door!'

Claudette screamed when she heard the next massive blows of the hammer against the thin wooden door. The panels started to buckle and splinter. The blows came heavier and faster. The window frame dug into her as she tried to push her way through. She chanced a look back just as a whole panel of the door split open and crashed to the bathroom floor. An arm came through the opening searching for the latch. She almost froze with panic. The window was too small! She was going to die here. She made one last effort and the frosted glass shattered, covering her with shards of glass. But with the windowpane gone, the frame was now pliable. She pushed hard at it and it gave way. Suddenly, the bathroom door burst open. She was halfway through the window as the figure entered the bathroom. Claudette pulled up her legs but felt a strong hand grab one of her ankles. A vice-like grip pulled her back.

She kicked and screamed and for a brief moment the hand let go. She plunged headfirst to the fire escape outside and staggered as she tried to stand up. The tall figure was right behind her as it climbed onto the toilet cistern. Claudette fled down the stairs, screaming. She held onto the railing and slid most of the way to the lane at the bottom. Swanston Street was only one hundred metres in front of her. She started to run, dodging skip bins and rubbish strewn about in the laneway. Her lungs were burning as she neared the main road. She gulped the air down. Finally, she made Swanston Street and chanced a look behind her. No one was there!

* * *

In Nick's office Claudette was still shaking as Nick held her tight. Pete Drury was with them.

'Did you get a look at who it was?' Drury asked.

Claudette shook her head. 'I couldn't see …' she gulped, '… had a ski mask on.'

Drury wasn't finished. 'Was there a weapon?'

'Yes … a hammer … a huge, huge hammer!' Claudette started to cry.

'Look Pete, she's traumatised,' Nick said, 'she just needs to calm down a bit!'

'I know, mate, but we've got a massive problem here, and I need to get this guy!'

Rosalie fussed around Claudette. She gently took her hand and led her out into the reception area.

Drury strode over to the window and stared out at Swanston Street below.

'How'd they get in the lift?' Drury asked.

Nick slumped down in his chair. 'Dunno!' Then added, 'Jesus, Pete, three break-ins in four days!'

'Yeah I know,' Drury said rubbing his brow. 'You been handin' out keys, or something?' Drury cocked his head to one side. 'You know: the girlfriend, the ex-wife – somebody else, maybe?'

'No!' Nick blurted out. 'I'm the only one with a key to the lift.' He stopped mid-stream. 'Except … that is …'

'Who?' Drury asked.

'Hendrix. The maintenance guy. He's got a key to all the apartments in the block. But he only ever uses it after he calls me, you know, to make sure it's okay to go in.'

Pete Drury leant forward. 'So where are Hendrix's digs?

Nick looked at Drury. 'Two doors down. He lives in the basement, under the footpath. Gets daylight from those frosted glass pavement blocks, but I guess he's got electricity,' Nick shrugged as he spoke.

'Sounds fancy!' Drury said sarcastically. 'Let's call on Mr Hendrix.'

Out on Flinders Street, Nick showed Drury where Hendrix lived. Drury noticed that the door leading down to the basement was already partially open. It creaked as he pushed against it. He searched for a light switch but couldn't find one. He took a torch out of his coat pocket and turned it on.

'Mr Hendrix!' Drury yelled from the top stair.

There was no answer.

'Hendrix?' he shouted.

Nick stood next to Drury and stared down into the dark basement. It reminded him of his recurring dream. It looked just like the tunnel he was running down trying to get away from whoever, or whatever, was chasing him. He hesitated and nearly jumped out of his skin when Drury grabbed his shoulder and said, 'After you,' and pointed downstairs.

Nick turned on the torch app of his mobile phone and started down the stairs. As he reached the basement floor Drury left him and began searching. The only noise was the muffled sound of footsteps overhead and the occasional rumble of a passing tram. Their torchlights crisscrossed in the gloom. Down in Hendrix's den there was stuff everywhere. There was a table and two chairs and a poster on the wall covered in dust. Then Nick's foot caught on something and he stumbled. He put his hands out to break his fall and found himself touching something hard and cold. When he looked closer he could see it was a body.

'Pete, over here!'

Drury swung his torch around and found Nick.

'Down there,' Nick said and pointed.

Drury shone the torch towards the floor. Hendrix's body was crammed into a corner of the basement. His arms were stretched out above his head where he'd clearly tried to defend himself. His face was a bloodied mash. Drury tried for a pulse.

'I'll call an ambulance!' Nick said.

Drury shook his head. 'Too late for an ambulance, mate! Your maintenance man is very, very dead.'

28

HIDEOUT

Tyson climbed back underneath the overpass at Oakleigh Station. He'd found a cranny there that provided shelter of some sort during the day; it was a place where he could hide and still watch what was happening. At night he went back to the male toilets where he'd forced his way in. It was cold, cramped and dark but at least he was sheltered from the elements. Alex hated it. It reminded him of being pushed into the background. But he knew he would just have to live with it. It was what Tyson wanted.

Alex came forward again. 'C-c-can we g-go back h-h-home now?'

'No!' Tyson hissed. 'We're not going anywhere right now! We've got someone we need to visit! Besides, we can't go home. They'll be looking for us there, idiot!'

Alex whimpered and moved back into the background.

Tyson took another bite of a hamburger and looked out onto the railway tracks as a late afternoon Pakenham line train slowly pulled into the station. He ducked down as the passengers disembarked. He felt in his pocket and found only a couple of coins – not enough for another meal. He would have to wait until after dark and rob someone else. It had now been two days since he'd mugged the last one. The guy put up a reasonable fight but was no match for Tyson, who'd watched him get off the train and head into the Junction Hotel just across the road from the station. Tyson waited in the dark for more than an hour until finally the man left the pub and crossed the road in front of some empty shops. Tyson ambushed him there. The drunk put up a good fight, but with a belly full of booze he eventually tired and slumped to the ground. Tyson punched the guy a number of times while he was down. There was blood everywhere. Then he took his wallet and was disappointed to see it only contained twenty bucks and no cards.

He watched as one of the last passengers left the platform. It was a pretty young girl with small boobs. Alex came forward. She reminded him of the girl he had asked to be his girlfriend – the dead girl! His mind also drifted back to Nurse Desiree. He wanted to see her again too!

Tyson pushed him back. 'Forget her! We're gonna find Portman Street tonight. Gonna see where Dr Shelton hangs out!'

'I-I'm s-s-scared though! W-what if the p-p-police f-f-find us?'

'You're weak Alex, piss weak! I'm too smart for them. Besides, I'm gonna find that bastard Shelton. Show him how much the procedure hurt! I'm gonna hurt him – hurt him *real* bad!'

He took another bite of the burger and watched as the girl walked up the overpass. She seemed to look down at him for a moment. He ducked back a bit but made sure he could still see her as she walked up the ramp. Her legs seemed to get longer and longer and her skirt shorter and shorter. He had to admit, she was very pretty, but there was no time to follow her now. He had a job to do!

29

NIGHT-TIME VISITOR

Jeffrey Shelton sat sweating in his consulting room in the late evening. The conditions were unbearable. He removed his glasses and wiped the sweat out of his eyes before he replaced them and flipped over another page of Alex Downton's file. He wondered where the hell he could be. With Downton gone, escaped in fact, and not even half the set of ECT treatments completed, he had nothing. He needed Downton back at Aimtree to complete the full set, something that could possibly take a year or more. He desperately needed it to be done so he could finish his research papers and prove that the method – *his method* as he now thought of it – was successful. The problem was that if the medical board found out now about what he'd been doing, he'd be reprimanded. His reputation would be in tatters – he might even be prosecuted. He had to find Downton, or at least tell that private investigator where he might be, so *he* could catch him.

He took the file with him as he got up and walked into the empty lounge room that doubled as the reception area, hoping it might not be as stuffy in there. He walked over to a window and pushed it open. The wind picked up and a brief squall blew through the room, dragging the curtains outside into the night as it raced away. The air was hot and heavy. Crickets sang and every now and then branches from the low garden bushes scraped noisily against the window as they were flung about by the unruly night air.

He opened a cupboard, took out a glass and poured himself a generous amount of Scotch. He sat back in a tattered lounge chair and stared out at the night. It was starting to stir. In the distance dry lightning lit up the menacing dark clouds. The storm was on its way!

He opened the file, reread his notes and slowly shook his head.

> *Research note: The method of combining the ECT with a mild sedative was working well – the patient did not complain during the treatment*

(He failed to mention that Downton strained continuously against the leather tie-down straps when the electrodes were applied. But that was just the body reacting to the electricity. To be expected, he thought. There was also no reference to Dr Paul Reading who had proposed this treatment at a conference some twelve months ago.)

Research note: The day after the procedure the patient appeared to be calm and reserved. There was no evidence of "switching"

(There was also no reference to the incident between Downton and his mother and the need for the orderly to calm Downton down after one of the treatments.)

Research note: After six months the patient appeared to be stronger and coping with the procedure well

(He didn't mention the possibility that Tyson, the stronger, more violent personality, seemed to have taken over and was therefore better able to cope with the treatment.)

Research note: The patient's social skills had improved significantly. It was critically important that the patient be seen by the same nurse and doctor prior to, during and after the treatment, to build trust and put the patient at ease at all times

(At this stage he hadn't mentioned Downton's fascination with Nurse Thompson's small breasts. Alex had told Shelton they reminded him of a dead girlfriend of his, and also his stepsister Jessica. These facts were complicated. Shelton decided he would include details of this aspect of Downton's personality in his papers at a later date, but noted at the moment it would require further investigation.)

Shelton removed his glasses and placed them on the small table next to him. He swirled the whisky around in the glass and took a sip. 'Things were going so well,' he muttered to himself.

Downton was his ticket to fame and fortune. He just had to be found!

Outside the wind picked up again and howled underneath the eaves. The bushes outside kept tap, tap, tapping against the window. Shelton got up and was about to pull the curtains back inside when the lights flickered then went out. The house was immediately plunged into darkness. He stood in the pitch black trying to get his bearings. He turned towards the window where a faint light from the summer night threw dark shadows in the garden outside. The trees began to bend as another strong gust raced across the front of the house. In the distance lightning once more lit up the jet-black sky followed quickly by the deep rumble of thunder.

He jumped at a sound. Was it glass breaking? It sounded like it came from the back of the house.

He turned towards the corridor, felt for the side table and put his glass down. As he did, the window behind him splintered. A huge crack ran from the top all the way to the bottom. The wind intensified. He could hear the tiles on the roof shifting, lifting and falling with each massive gust. Shelton's heart was thumping. He felt uneasy. His eyes were becoming used to the darkened room and he was about to move when he heard the floorboards creak at the other end of the house. He stayed dead still.

Was someone in the house? His mind began to race. He held his breath and strained his ears, trying to hear over the incessant howl of the wind. The creaking noise came again and this time he was sure he heard a footstep. He started slowly walking towards the corridor when he caught his shin on the coffee table. He slowly inched around it.

'Someone there?' he called out loud.

There was no reply, just the wind outside, rising and falling. He moved a step closer to the corridor and as he did he heard the floorboards creak again. The footsteps were closer now. Someone was definitely there!

'Hello … hello … Who's there?' He spoke loudly but struggled to keep the tremor out of his voice.

Again, there was no reply. He was about to take another step when he heard what he thought was a voice. He stopped.

'Hello?' he shouted out.

It was definitely a voice he heard. He was sure of it! Shelton's heart was almost jumping out of his chest. He managed to take another step towards the corridor when a tall, dark figure appeared before him, blocking his path.

A voice snarled. 'I said … hi, Dr Shelton.'

Shelton was practically panting now. His voice trembled,

'Who-who are you?'

The tall figure moved forward.

'What do you want?' Shelton strained to see who it was, but it wasn't possible in the dark.

'Looked like you were trying to go somewhere, Dr Shelton,' the menacing voice growled.

Shelton didn't reply. He was too terrified to move. The voice was familiar – very familiar – but he just couldn't place it.

The tall figure took a step forward and hissed, 'It's too late for running, Dr Shelton – way too late for running!'

He shivered as the sweat froze on his body. For a fleeting moment he had a crazy hope that it was someone from the SES, or maybe a neighbour.

The dark figure took another step forward. Shelton stepped backwards, tripped on his chair and sat down heavily.

'The procedure, Dr Shelton … The procedure hurts!'

Oh my God! he thought. It was Tyson!

'It fuckin' hurts bad Dr Shelton!'

'I'm sorry Alex … ahh, Tyson, but you never called out or—'

'Not possible!' The tall figure took another step then screamed like a banshee. 'IT'S NOT POSSIBLE TO CALL OUT DURING THE PROCEDURE, DR SHELTON!'

Shelton was now very worried. He was in a vulnerable position. He had to think quickly. 'Perhaps … perhaps I'll reduce the intensity,' he said, thinking on his feet. 'That'll make it better!'

'No! You're going to stop it altogether!' the figure said.

'But I can't. It's good for you! It's helping you to get better!'

'Buuullllll shiiiiitttt!' came the voice.

Lightning lit up the sky and for a brief moment, Shelton clearly saw the tall figure standing over him. His eyes opened wide and the breath caught in his throat as he recognised the face.

Thunder crashed loudly, so close now that it shook the walls.

The hammer swung down in a quick deadly arc. It bounced sideways off Shelton's skull and caught his shoulder, smashing it. He screamed in pain, slid off the chair and began crawling along the floor. He started whimpering.

'I can help! I'll make sure it doesn't hurt anymore! I-I promise!'

'Yes ... you *will*, Dr Shelton!' the tall figure screeched.

The hammer found him again, this time on a leg. Shelton shrieked and rolled onto his back.

'Stop, for god's sake, stop! I'll stop the procedure, I'll—'

He looked up into the demonic eyes as the hammer slammed into his forehead and everything went black.

* * *

Shelton's bloodied head bounced along the wooden floorboards as he was dragged by his feet to the back of the house. The door to the bathroom was opened and he was hauled in. The tall figure then hogtied Shelton, making sure his hands and feet were drawn together and pulled up tight behind his back. A cloth was stuffed in his mouth and secured in place. He was then manhandled upwards to the edge of the bath, lifted and bundled in. He thumped down into the bath on his back and came around as the cold water tap was turned on and the water began to swirl around him. He was pushed to one side as the plug was fitted into place.

In the dark of the bathroom Shelton's eyes darted around. He looked pleadingly at the tall figure. He struggled, but it was useless, he could hardly move. The noise of the water rushing into the bath was incessant. His hands began to ache as the cold water flowed over them. Soon his back was saturated.

The tall figure walked outside to the meter box, flicked the power safety switch back to the ON position and the house lit up again.

Shelton heard footsteps on the floorboards as the figure re-entered the house. The bathroom door was shoved open, the light switch turned on and a two-bar electric heater from Shelton's office was placed on the edge of the bath.

'Now you'll see how much the electricity hurts, Dr Shelton.'

Shelton watched, terrified, as the heater was plugged in and turned on. The radiant bars immediately began to burn a bright red. He squirmed and thrashed in the water. But as hard as he tried he couldn't get out. The bath was now half full and despite the heat of the night, he started to shiver as the cold of the water seeped into his body.

He kept looking back and forth between the heater and the tall dark figure standing over him. He was trying to beg, but with the gag in place it was impossible, he could only mumble.

The heater was pushed closer to the water. Now it was teetering on the edge.

'I wouldn't struggle if I were you, Dr Shelton. The more you struggle, the closer to the edge it gets.'

Shelton could feel the heat. It was burning his face. He mumbled something behind the gag and tears pricked his eyes. He looked up, praying that the heater wouldn't be pushed in.

He shivered uncontrollably. The water now covered his chest and was up to his neck. He craned forward trying to lift his head but it quickly reached his mouth. He choked as he sucked water in. He struggled upward again, desperate to keep the water away from his nose.

The tall figure knelt down beside him and in a soft, calm voice said, 'You're wondering, aren't you, Dr Shelton, why you're all trussed up like that?' Hair covering Shelton's forehead was gently pushed to one side. 'Well *now*, Dr Shelton, you know how it feels to be tied down and not able to move.'

A finger was placed on the top of Shelton's head and

pushed him under. He strained and writhed against the ropes holding him in place. The finger was removed and he bobbed back up and began to suck in great gulps of air.

The heater was pushed a little closer to the edge, so close to Shelton now that an ugly red blister formed on his forehead. He whimpered.

'And you wonder why you've got a gag?' The tall figure looked at him and nodded. 'Well, Dr Shelton, it's so you can't scream! You see, it's not possible to scream when you get the procedure, Dr Shelton. IT'S – JUST – NOT – POSSIBLE – TO – SCREAM!'

The water flowed over Shelton's mouth again. He fought to keep his nose clear.

The tall figure bent over him and said in a soft voice, 'Goodbye, Dr Shelton. Don't worry. This won't hurt a bit! Not – one – little – bit.'

The heater was pushed into the bath. It crackled loudly as the water reached the glowing bars. The current surged through the water and found Shelton's body. He convulsed violently, sending up great waves of water. He did try to scream, but his throat was so constricted that nothing came out. He thrashed around uncontrollably. The intense pain registered so completely in his eyes, they looked like they were going to explode out of his head.

Within seconds, the bathroom was plunged back into darkness as the heater shorted the electricity circuit. Shelton's tortured head slid below the waterline. Bubbles escaped his nose. A hand was placed on the top of his head again, but this time it held him under. Shelton's struggles were minimal now. In a final gush, a stream of bubbles escaped his nose as his body reached its final death throes.

The cold water continued to run and the bath overflowed. Water cascaded down its sides and rushed along the floor.

From across the road a man walking his dog watched as a tall person dressed in a hoodie left Dr Shelton's house and hurried down the street. He was concerned. He lived in the same street as the doctor and knew that he never saw any of his patients this time of night. He also saw the lights in the doctor's house come on and then within minutes go off again; it seemed strange. And the front door was left wide open. He put his hand over his mouth and stared at the house. He couldn't be sure, but it looked like water was running out of the front door.

Overhead a bolt of lightning lit up the dark clouds and thunder cracked down. The dog began to bark. He looked up at the dark brooding sky and decided it was time to go home. The storm seemed very close now.

He picked up his small dog and carried it in his arms as he strode along the street to his house. When he told his wife what he'd seen she convinced him to call the police.

30

THE STORM

At six o'clock the next night in the front bar of Young & Jackson, Nick decided to have one more pot before he went upstairs for his usual steak and chips in Chloe's Brasserie. He could take his time as he was sleeping in his office while the forensics team were still in his apartment looking for anything that could help identify the intruder. They told him they'd be there at least another day, so he made the office as comfortable as he could. Rosalie had offered to let Claudette stay at her place until she could move back in with Nick, so he was confident they'd both be safe.

He watched the news as he sipped on the ice-cold beer.

Heading up tonight's bulletin is the brutal murder of Doctor Jeffrey Shelton, a well-respected psychiatrist, in his office in Oakleigh. Police have confirmed that Shelton was murdered some time last night. It appears he was beaten about the head with a blunt instrument, then placed in a bath of cold water where

*his death came about from either electrocution
or drowning. The coroner has been contacted
and a thorough examination of the body will
be conducted to determine the exact cause of
death.*

*At this stage the police forensics team is on
site and police are not saying if they have any
leads or known suspects.*

*We will be the first to keep you informed of
any developments as soon as they are to hand.*

'Jesus!' Nick whispered to himself.

*In other news, the heavy storm slowly moving in
from the west is likely to hit Melbourne tonight.
People are advised to stay home and secure
anything that could be picked up by the wind.
There is a strong possibility of flash flooding in
the city and surrounding suburbs.*

By 8:00pm, Nick was back in his office. He stood up at the window and watched as the hot northerly tore down Swanston Street. Across the road at St Paul's Cathedral trees bent and shook, threatening to be ripped out of the ground. Loose papers skittled along the street, tearing through Fed Square before being thrust high in the air and tossed about on their way down St Kilda Road towards the Shrine. Groups of people waiting at the tram stops outside Flinders Street Station covered themselves as best they could as clouds of dust and grit swirled and were flung about. Tram-lines swung erratically in the strong wind. The windows in

Nick's office rattled insanely with every heavy gust.

Along the beaches of Port Phillip Bay, the savage wind whipped up giant waves. Rocks from the sea walls lining the foreshore were picked up and thrown across the esplanade. Sand, like bullets, was hurled against the houses, and palm trees lining the pavements bent at crazy angles. All along the coastline houses were battered. In some neighbourhoods, roofs were completely torn off, exposing their contents to the elements. Those poor individuals caught out in the storm stood little chance. The wind was so ferocious it knocked people off their feet. Ambulances were called out in droves to tend to numerous injuries. Emergency departments were packed and hospitals overrun.

Back in the CBD the first squall hit. Intermittent raindrops, hot and stinging, sizzled and bounced along the city streets. The smell of rain on baking hot roads filled the air. Soon huge raindrops began to fall, teeming down. The noise of them striking the roads and footpaths was deafening. Torrents of water began to run. Gutters overflowed as the heavy storm clouds dumped their load. Tree branches started to crack and break. Lightning streaked across the Melbourne sky as thunder boomed and reverberated along the city streets, rocking the office towers.

The lights in Nick's office flickered briefly then went out. For a moment it was pitch black, but then the battery backup on his laptop kicked in. The computer screen came to life and lit up the office with an eerie blue glow. The message icon in the bottom right-hand corner began counting email messages. It finished at twenty-five. He clicked on the email icon and put in his username and password. He clicked on the last email and read it:

> Hey Jarratt, you loser. Someone's gonna get it
> tonight – guess who – guess who – guess who –
> guess who – guess who – guess who …

Just then, Nick's mobile phone rang.

'Jarratt,' Nick said as he covered the opposite ear trying to block out the noise of the storm.

'Mr Jarratt, it's Jessica Downton.'

'Yes Miss Downton?'

'Mr Jarratt I've found something in the house that might interest you. It might help you to find Alex.'

'What is it?'

'It's a diary Alex made with all sorts of pictures in it. It talks of places he went when his mother was … entertaining a man.'

Nick was stunned by her last comment and remained silent for a moment.

'Can you bring it in tomorrow?' he asked.

'Mr Jarratt. This might help you to find him tonight. He'll be terrified in weather like this! Can't you come and take a look?' She paused, 'Please, Mr Jarratt, I'm so worried about him.'

Nick took another look out the window. The storm was really moving in.

'All right, I'll be there as soon as I can,' he said reluctantly, and hung up.

As soon as he walked out onto Swanston Street the wind grabbed him and threatened to send him flying. He was saturated in a moment. He glanced up along the street but turned away as the rain stung his face in a thousand places. He turned his back and made it around the corner into Flinders Street where he was met by the full force of the brutal conditions. He stooped and bent his head low as he fought his way to his apartment block. He inserted the key into the lock and waited while the barred metal gate to the underground car park slowly lifted. He walked down the concrete ramp and found his car.

The drive over to Hawthorn was horrendous. The wind threatened to throw the car off the road. The windscreen wipers had little effect on the torrential rain; it was only the gale-force wind that blew the water off the windscreen long enough for him to see.

He pulled up in front of the Downton house and got out. Rain bucketed down. Lightning lit up the sky and thunder boomed out simultaneously. He leapt up the front stairs two at a time and rang the doorbell. He looked back over his shoulder at the weather and waited for Jessica to open the door.

'Oh, Mr Jarratt, thank you so much for coming out in such atrocious weather! Come in, please.'

Nick walked through into the huge foyer, dripping wet.

'You can dry off in here.'

She showed Nick to a powder room off to the side. He went in, found a towel and ran it through his wet hair. He dried his clothes as best he could. He walked back to where she was standing in the foyer.

'So, Miss Downton, what did you find of Alex's?'

She handed him a tattered book. It had weird drawings on the front. He opened it up and began to read the various scribbles:

> 'Hate Victor – don't like Naughty Boy – I
> want a puppy – love Jessica – don't hurt my
> Mum.'

The scribbles went on and on.

'So how does this help?' Nick asked a little peeved.

'A few more pages in there's a reference to the wine cellar downstairs. He says there's something special of his down there. Something that he hides there.'

Nick looked up at her and then flipped through the pages.

'Show me where,' he said, and handed her the diary.

Jessica turned a few pages until she found it. 'Here,' she said and pointed to an entry. 'I'm not sure what it means but it could be important. It might be something he comes back for, or it might help you to find him.'

Nick hesitated and frowned.

'It's something he has in the cellar. I thought we should have a look,' she urged. 'But I'm a bit scared, Mr Jarratt. I don't know what we'll find.'

Nick was apprehensive but decided to follow this lead. 'Okay, show me the cellar.'

They walked to a door off to the side of the foyer. She

unlocked and opened it.

'That's it,' she said and pointed down into the darkness.

'You come down here often?' Nick said.

'No, I hate it! It's too scary for me! My father's wine se-lection is there, but I never venture down.'

'Did you ever see Alex come down here?'

'No. But I guess he did. That's what it says in his diary.'

Nick hesitated.

'The light switch is just to the right,' she said, prompting him.

Nick took a deep breath, found the switch and turned it on. A bright light lit up a narrow staircase and the vast expanse of the underground room.

'Wow! Significant!' he remarked.

They started down the dozen or so stairs.

'I don't like it here, Mr Jarratt. I'm going back up,' Jessica said.

'Okay,' Nick said. 'I'll have a quick look around.'

The sound of the storm became muffled the further Nick went down. He got to the last step, then stepped off onto the cold concrete floor. He was greeted by row after row of wines all stacked neatly in wooden racks. The first two racks looked like whites followed by four more of reds. He walked around them and looked at the walls. Someone had scrawled in large red letters:

> 'He's not stupid!' 'You are not helping!' 'The bitch deserved it – he likes her more than me!'

Nick jumped when his mobile rang. It was Pete Drury. The line was terrible.

'Yeah, Pete – what's up?' Nick said, half yelling.

'We've got …' The line broke up then came back to life. '… ownton.'

'What? I'm sorry Pete I can hardly hear you.'

'I said, we've got your boy Downton … Alex Downton.'

Nick was stunned. 'Where, when?'

Static buzzed loudly. Nick moved to another part of the cellar.

'Yesterday afternoon. Got a tip-off from a girl who said someone was under the overpass at Oakleigh Station pervin' up her skirt. Boys in blue from Oakleigh cop shop got him! Didn't put up a great fight apparently. We've got him now and are sendin' him back to Aimtree tomorrow.'

Nick was speechless.

'You still there?' Drury shouted.

'Yeah, yeah … just a little surprised!'

Drury went on. 'Suppose you heard that Dr Shelton was murdered last night?'

'Yeah I saw it on the TV at the pub … beaten about the head and put in a bath!'

'Yeah, bashed senseless all right! Then dragged to the back of the house to the bathroom. Big trail of blood …' The line cut out momentarily and then back in, '… ran the water and threw in an electric heater. Coroner's looking at it now.'

'Jesus,' said Nick. 'So, he got to Shelton before you guys picked him up?'

'No! He was ... in custody by then!' The static blared. 'Someone else ... did the deed on Shelton!'

'Who? From the TV report it was the same MO – well the blunt instrument part! Who else would want to kill Shelton?'

Drury didn't answer him. Instead he said, 'Just wait ... it gets better!'

The line cut out again. Nick moved closer to the centre of the cellar and pressed the phone hard against his ear.

'You know I told ya we found Victor, Alex's stepfather ... dead ... head bashed in!'

'Yeah,' Nick yelled trying to make himself heard.

'Well, it looks like it couldn't have been Downton that killed him – he was in Oakleigh then. Least that's how it appears at the moment. So we did some more diggin' around.'

Nick stood there stunned and didn't speak.

'We've made some inquiries around his stepsister,' Drury yelled.

'Jessica?' Nick asked. 'I'm with her now!' he shouted into the phone.

'Nick! She hasn't been seen at her job in the pharmacy for weeks!' Drury was now shouting as well.

Nick took this in. 'So ... maybe she quit,' he said, not really convinced of what he was saying.

'Nick ... there is no Jessica Downton!'

'What?'

A crash of thunder echoed in the cellar.

'It's Jessica Haslock. Same surname as her father – Victor Haslock.'

The line broke up again.

'Pete, I don't understand!'

'Nick, we can't find Helen Downton either, but thank God Rosalie is on the ball.'

'Rosalie – what do you mean?'

The line cut out and then back in with crystal clarity.

'Well, you know how she fixed the CCTV in your office.'

'Yeah,' Nick said, not sure where this was going.

'Well, she rang me and said she was getting suspicious of Jessica Downton. So I asked her if she had any closed circuit vision of Downton. She emailed me some images of her later that day, and there was a pretty good face scan we used.'

'And?' Nick was starting to get agitated.

'Got the team here to check it out! No criminal record, but one of the switched-on uni grads we hire these days sent her photo to the Aussie passport office and asked them to have a look and see if she had a passport.'

'Well? Jesus, Pete! Just tell me what you found will ya, this line is really bad!'

'We've got a match. It turns out it's not Jessica Downton who's been coming to see you. It's *Helen* Downton, the mother! Looks like she's taken Jessica Haslock's identity!'

Nick stood there, dumbfounded. He could feel the hairs on the back of his neck stand on end as shivers ran up his spine.

'So, where's Jessica?' Nick asked.

'Good question!'

The line broke up again as the storm raged outside. Then Drury's voice cut back in. 'Nick, where are you now?'

'With Jessica Downton, at her mother's place.'

'What?'

'At Helen Downton's place!' Nick yelled.

Drury's voice became very faint. '… in this weather?'

'Yeah.' The line broke off then came back. '… she found his diary which led us to the cellar…'

'In the cellar?' Drury asked incredulously.

Nick didn't answer as a crack of thunder filtered down into the room. He heard: 'Nick … problem… get out of there now!'

The line cut out then back in.

'Why … what's goin' on?'

'… get out Nick! It's not Alex! It's not – who did you say his other personality was?'

'Tyson!' Nick yelled, looking towards the staircase that ran back up to the ground floor.

'… we think it might … been the mother all along!'

Just then there was an enormous clap of thunder and the lights in the cellar went out, leaving the room in pitch black. At the top of the stairs the door slammed shut.

'Shit!' Nick said as he groped around, trying to get his bearings.

'What … Nick … you okay? … Nick! …Nick! …' Drury was shouting down the phone.

But the call disconnected, leaving Nick with only the silence of a dead phone line.

31

HELEN DOWNTON

Nick stood in the cellar trying to remember where the wine racks were. It was a full minute before he remembered the torch feature on his phone and he switched it on. He moved towards the stairs, then something caught his eye in the far corner. It was a bundle of blankets tied together with what looked like dressing gown cords. He walked over and nudged it with his foot. It was heavy. He lifted a loose part of the blanket. Underneath was a thick black plastic wrap. He pulled more of the blanket away, exposing more of the plastic. A faint rank smell filled the air. Nick put the phone down and in the semi-gloom he continued pulling the black plastic away. Finally, he saw small wisps of human hair. As he removed more of the plastic the stench got worse. Soon he exposed the battered and decaying head of a young woman.

Nick stared at the corpse. No doubt, he thought, he'd found the remains of Jessica Haslock.

There was a noise at the top of the stairs. The door creaked as it opened. Nick remained totally silent and watched as a tall figure, holding a torch, appeared on the top step.

'Mr Jarratt?'

Nick didn't answer. He quickly turned off the phone torch. The voice came again, but this time much deeper.

'Mr Jarratt!' There was complete silence. 'I can hear you Mr Jarratt!'

Nick remained silent, then his heart froze when he heard her again. 'It's too late for running, Mr Jarratt! Way too late for running!' He felt paralysed by fear.

'I'll find you, Mr Jarratt. Please come out! I need to pay you for your time!'

In the dark Nick desperately tried to remember the location of the wine racks. He slowly crawled towards where he thought they were, put out his hand and touched the cold rounded glass bottom of a bottle.

'I see you've found her … I can smell the bitch!'

Helen Downton began to descend the stairs. She swept the torch light over the cellar floor.

'She was nosey, Mr Jarratt! Always fussing over Alex, my boy Alex! He loved *me*, not *her*!

Nick tried to not make any sound.

'You know she tried to seduce him. Alex told me he liked her because she showed him her tiny tits Mr Jarratt! Can you believe that!'

Helen Downton came down another few stairs. Nick

chanced a quick glance to see where she was. His stomach clenched with fear when he saw she was holding a hammer and wearing those beautiful white gloves. No wonder forensics never found any fingerprints, he thought.

'No good hiding, Mr Jarratt. There is nowhere to hide!'

Nick heard her scuff along the floor and then speak in a low guttural voice: 'No sense running, Mr Jarratt – it's way, way too late for running!' She was still shuffling forward.

'You rejected me, Mr Jarratt! You could have had me, but you refused!' She started to walk beside the first wine rack.

'Instead, you took up with that that blonde hussy and let her stay in your apartment!' she shrieked, 'You chose her over me!' She stopped and started searching around with her torch beam.

'Why do you think I came to see you, Mr Jarratt? Of all the men I could have chosen, I chose you!'

Nick stayed perfectly silent.

'I knew you were lonely, Mr Jarratt. I saw you a long time ago eating alone in that hotel night after night. Then I watched you set up your office in that rundown building.'

She paused, still looking for him.

'You're a fool, Mr Jarratt, keeping that bitch in your apartment! Well, I almost got her didn't I?'

Her breathing was coming in gasps. She started talking to herself. 'Yes,' she whispered, 'I almost got that bitch. I almost got her!'

Nick saw that she was swinging the hammer back and

forth.

'You've frustrated me, Mr Jarratt. Frustrated me for far too long! You refused to find my boy, you preferred to eat lunch with that stupid fat cop friend of yours instead of looking for my boy!'

Nick thanked God he'd spoken to Drury when he had.

'What sort of man are you, Mr Jarratt?'

Nick slowly drew one of the wine bottles out of the rack as quietly as he could.

'I suppose you're wondering about the others. That bitch in South Melbourne! She was supposed to be looking after Alex in Aimtree, but he told me he liked her better than *me*! He liked her because she reminded him of Jessica – the slut! He said he liked to look at her small tits when she wasn't looking. I hated her! I took care of that bitch!'

She came further down the row of wine towards Nick.

'Then the other two, those two in the driveway. Alex told me they laughed at him! Well, they didn't laugh at him for long, Mr Jarratt! I gave Alex the hammer, but in the end he didn't use it – *I had to!* I told him *that's how you do it when someone laughs at you!* My poor boy got the blame for that one, but it was necessary. It was a learning experience for him!'

She shuffled further along. 'He also got the blame for Mrs Ashby, that stupid old woman walking that bloody dog that never shut up! She caused my boy to end up in Aimtree, Mr Jarratt. That old cow also deserved it!'

She was looking behind the wine racks.

'And, oh yes! Dr Shelton! Do you know how much that procedure hurt my boy, Mr Jarratt?' She paused as she continued looking. 'Of course, you don't! Alex told me, no, he begged me, to make Dr Shelton stop, but he refused! So … I made sure he wasn't going to hurt my boy anymore, Mr Jarratt! He'll never hurt my boy again. I made sure he got a taste of the electricity.'

She moved from one side of the wine racks to the other.

'I should have got that nurse Desiree Thompson too, the whore! Alex kept looking at her boobs, he said he wanted her to be his girlfriend! Can you imagine that, Mr Jarratt! Alex, with a girlfriend?'

She gave a high-pitched crazy scream.

Nick drew back the bottle and hurled it at the opposite wall. The sound of it smashing was deafening. He quickly grabbed another bottle as a weapon and drew it back. He gasped as he saw she was almost on top of him.

She swung the hammer down and it glanced off Nick's forehead.

'Ahh!' he yelled as he slumped to the floor.

'I can't let you live, Mr Jarratt. Too many loose ends!'

She swung the hammer again and this time it caught Nick on the left shoulder. The pain was instant and excruciating as the massive hammer head struck home.

'Oh no!' he shouted.

Nick rolled to one side and slid out of the way but she was quickly onto him. 'Too late for running, Mr Jarratt! Way, way too late for running!'

She swung the hammer again. Nick put up his hands to take the blow but it glanced off and struck his knee. He felt paralysed as he lost all feeling in his leg. She came at him again swinging wildly. As hard as Nick tried, he could not get up off the floor. The wine bottle in his hand was useless.

He cowered away as best he could and ended up next to the decaying body of Jessica Haslock. Helen Downton walked over to him screaming. Her face was screwed up into an insane mask of fury. She was babbling and held the hammer up high, ready to strike the final blow.

'Niiiick!' A voice came from the top of the stairs.

Helen Downton turned around.

'Down here!' Nick screamed.

He used the wall to prop himself up on one leg, lifted the wine bottle and hit her. The blow glanced off her head and crashed into her shoulder. She staggered and shrieked in agony.

Drury shone his torch in Nick's direction. It lit up Helen Downton.

'Helen Downton! Police! Put the hammer down!' Drury yelled. 'Put it down or I will shoot!'

She stood in the middle of the cellar and faced Drury, glass shards filled her hair and red wine dripped down her clothes. Slowly she let the hammer fall to the floor. Nick watched as her demeanour slowly changed. Her face turned from an ugly scowl to a friendly smile as a different, softer personality took hold.

'No need to shoot, officer, I'm not Helen. I'm Jessica.

We're all friends here aren't we, Mr Jarratt?' she said as she turned and faced Nick.

'We're all just really good friends.'

32

AFTERMATH

A week later

'How are your injuries goin'?' Drury asked as he stretched back in Nick's visitor's chair.

'Yeah okay, I guess. I'll live,' Nick said and gingerly ran the tips of his fingers along the lumpy red graze on his forehead. He blew out his cheeks and then kept deleting the stack of emails. 'Never did find out why she was sending these!' he said.

'I think she was jealous of you and Claudette. Then you pissed her off mightily when you didn't come on to her!' Drury snickered. 'We found those in a sent file on a laptop she was using. Looks like it might have belonged to her husband originally. *Poor old Victor!*'

Drury got up and walked over to the window behind Nick's chair. He lit a cigarette and peered out at St Paul's Cathedral across the road. It would need major repairs after the battering it had taken from the storm. Then he laughed to himself.

'Tell you what, it was just as well you didn't do anything stupid. She sure didn't like her husbands!'

'How do you mean?' asked Nick.

'Once we got her to the station, she didn't hold back. She told us everything! We asked her about Victor. She confessed to that one as well. Said she went to his office block and snuck into the underground car park and waited for him to finish for the night. Poor bugger never stood a chance. She was pretty handy with that hammer!'

Drury took a deep draw on the cigarette and went on.

'She also told us of one we didn't know about – dude called Drew, her first husband. He copped it as well. Apparently he'd made threatening comments towards Alex. She said she wasn't gonna stand for that, so she spiked his dinner with some sort of anti-depression drug after one of his drinking sessions. Anyhow it must have knocked him out. She said she dragged him into the garage and propped him up in the driver's seat of his car, started it up and ran a hose from the exhaust into the window. The coroner's report mentioned there was a contusion to the back of that poor bugger's head as well, but he thought it was incidental and not important.' Drury sniffed and shook his head. 'Yeah mate, Helen Downton, just the sort of woman you'd want as a wife, hey!' He smiled and clapped Nick on the shoulder.

Nick winced then shook his head. His thoughts went back to the house where she'd tried to get him into the shower with her. He shivered involuntarily thinking just how lucky he'd been.

Drury took a long draw on his cigarette. 'Funny how she called herself Jessica, especially when she hated the girl so much!'

Nick nodded his head, thinking. 'You know when I saw Dr Shelton, he said that mental illness in the family ran hardest on the female side. When she "switched" in the cellar, I suspected she had the same condition as Alex. So perhaps ... just perhaps, she *was* Jessica some of the time.'

Drury looked out the window and shook his head and said, 'Strange!'

'Thanks again for gettin' me out of that cellar when you did, Pete!'

Drury smiled. 'Once again I saved your bacon!' he said and deliberately didn't smile. 'But Rosalie's the one you should really thank. If it wasn't for her, and her suspicions about Downton, you'd probably be in that cellar right now, all nicely tethered up and rotting alongside Jessica!'

'Yeah I guess you're right, mate. She is ... efficient ... even if a little annoying!'

'Funny,' Drury said, as he dragged in another lungful of smoke, 'that's exactly what her ex-husband says about her.'

Nick shook his head. 'Thanks, mate,' he said and flinched as he touched the lump on his knee. 'I owe you one.'

'Bullshit, mate! You owe me a lot more than one!' This time Drury did smile. 'You up to buying me lunch at Young & Jackson? We could look at Chloe again, remind us of some of the criminally insane we know!' He sniggered.

'Yeah sure, Pete, but you're gonna have to help me get there. This knee's still no good,' Nick said as he slowly spun around in his chair and tried to straighten out his leg.

'All right, anything that'll get me a free feed,' Drury said and smiled. 'And get something decent to drink this time. No more of that bloody house shiraz!'

* * *

Twelve months later

Helen Downton looked out of the window of her seclusion room on the third floor. The dinner, left by the nurse, stood on her small table, untouched. She walked over and checked the door handle again, like she'd done dozens of times before, but as per usual it was locked – from the outside.

She wondered which room her boy Alex was in. She would ask the nurse when she came back with milk and biscuits later on. At least she'd been allowed to keep her mobile phone. Hidden away in a secure app were three photos she wanted Alex to see. They were shots of nurse Audrey Withers lying dead on the floor of her lounge room with her bare breasts showing. She knew he liked to look at them, but she'd show Alex the bigger picture. Show him what happens when he likes other women more than her.

Then she "switched" momentarily and Jessica came forward.

'Alex is a good boy. He likes me! I tried to find him when he escaped from this dreadful place!'

Helen Downton pushed her back. 'He only likes looking at your boobs. He loves *me*. He loves only ME!'